TRUSTING
TOMORROW

Visit us at www.boldstrokesbooks.com

By the Author

From This Moment On

True Confessions

Missing

Trusting Tomorrow

TRUSTING TOMORROW

by
PJ Trebelhorn

2013

ISBN 10: 1-60282-891-1
ISBN 13: 978-1-60282-891-9

THIS TRADE PAPERBACK ORIGINAL IS PUBLISHED BY
BOLD STROKES BOOKS, INC.
P.O. BOX 249
VALLEY FALLS, NY 12185

FIRST EDITION: AUGUST 2013

CREDITS

EDITORS: VICTORIA OLDHAM AND CINDY CRESAP
PRODUCTION DESIGN: SUSAN RAMUNDO
COVER DESIGN BY SHERI (GRAPHICARTIST2020@HOTMAIL.COM)

Acknowledgments

First and foremost, I want to thank Len Barot and everyone at Bold Strokes Books for continuing to have faith in me. I'm so very proud to be a part of this wonderful family.

To my editor, Victoria Oldham, thank you for all you've done. A simple thank you doesn't seem to be enough for everything you've taught me, but it's all I have.

Hugh and Betty James, I want to thank you—for everything. You have no idea how much I appreciate your generosity and hospitality.

Susan and Harvey Campbell—I love you guys. Your friendship means more to me than I could ever put into words. And I love how supportive you are of my writing. Susan, you're the best canasta partner I could ever hope to have. And now the world knows Harvey and Cheryl cheat at cards.

Steven Cunningham, your information on the funeral director occupation was incredibly helpful, and I thank you for agreeing to sit down and answer all my questions.

And last, but certainly not least, I want to thank you, the reader. Without all of you there would be no reason for any of us to keep writing.

Dedication

For Cheryl, always

CHAPTER ONE

The keys in her pocket were a weight Logan Swift wasn't sure she could bear. She sat in her car outside the house, her forehead resting on the steering wheel. Her grip was so tight her knuckles were turning white. She refused to cry. Not only because it signified weakness, but it wouldn't do for someone in her profession. It was her job to help people through their grief, not give in to it herself.

She glanced up at the sky, thinking how appropriate it was for it to be so gray on this of all days. They were calling for snow later in the day. Her father had passed on his love of snow to Logan, but today the snow clouds did little to lift her mood.

Her anxiety level spiked when her cell phone vibrated on her hip. After taking a moment to steady her breathing, she answered the call.

"Yeah," she said almost inaudibly. She cleared her throat and decided to make another attempt. "Hello."

"Hey, Logan," said her younger brother Jack, his voice much more solemn than she was used to. "I just arrived at the funeral home. Where are you?"

"At the house." She glanced at the front steps of the double they had both grown up in. Even through the tears blurring her vision she could see the curtains were closed and the porch light had been left on, a testament to the fact her father hadn't planned on being home before dark the day before. She took in the white paint job, absently thinking it needed to be redone sometime soon. The frigid winters and hot, humid summers in northwestern Pennsylvania had caused the paint to begin peeling. Maybe she'd get vinyl siding put on rather than repainting. Regardless, it would have to wait until spring now, since winter was well on its way.

The house had originally been built as a huge single family home, but sometime in the fifties had been converted into a twin. A common wall separated the two houses in which the layout of one side mirrored the other. Her father had owned both halves and rented the other side out to the Colliers.

"How is it?"

"Still standing."

Jack chuckled. Logan cursed the fact he knew her so well. Knew she'd be sitting outside trying to talk herself into walking up those steps and going inside. Logan was surprised he'd managed to get home so quickly. She figured there'd be miles of red tape involved with the Cleveland Browns letting him come home for the funeral, but she was grateful he'd managed to get away because she really didn't think she'd be able to get through it on her own.

A curtain moved in a window on the other half of the double, and it caught Logan's eye, temporarily making her forget why she was there. Someone was spying on her. She knew it couldn't be Mr. or Mrs. Collier, because Henry, confined to a wheelchair, was most likely parked right in front of the television and not giving a hoot what was going on outside. His wife, Peggy, wasn't the type to be covert. If she wanted to know what was going on in the neighborhood, she'd damn well come out on the front porch and let you know you were being watched. And she'd likely have a shotgun at her side if she didn't know who you were.

Logan smiled in spite of the pain in her chest, because she loved those people like they were her own grandparents. They'd lived in the other half of the double since before she was born, and they'd been as involved in her upbringing as her own parents had been.

Her parents.

The thought brought her firmly back to the reason she was there. She sighed and closed her eyes again, her forehead back on the steering wheel, the phone still held to her ear by a hand she had a sudden urge to use to punch something.

"Let me guess," Jack said, his tone a strange mixture of teasing and grief of his own. "You're sitting out in the car staring at the house."

"Fuck, Jack, I can't do this," she said, choking back a sob. She was thirty-three years old for God's sake, and Jack was three years younger. They weren't supposed to be orphans, were they? Could you even be an orphan at her age? She sure as hell felt like she was. It was at times like these she was convinced there was no God. She never really believed in a higher power anyway, but damn it, she still *needed* her father. He was too young to be dead at the age of fifty-five. Her mother was only forty when she'd given in to the cancer which had ravaged her body almost fifteen years earlier. Logan had been convinced she'd never recover from her mother's death, but somehow she had. And now the pain of losing her was right there on the surface again with the loss of her father.

"Why don't you call Ernie in Riverside and have his people take over on this one?" Jack sounded as weary as she felt. His usual way was to try to make her laugh, and she would have given anything for him to be able to do it now, but she knew he could be serious when the situation called for it, and this one definitely did. "Nobody would blame you if you passed it off to someone else."

"Pass it off? Jesus, Jack, you make it sound so impersonal. No, I just need to get myself together and I'll be fine," she said, trying to reassure him as much as herself. She rubbed a hand over her face and sat back in the seat.

"You're probably lucky nobody's called the cops on you yet," Jack said in one of his attempts to lighten the mood.

"Everybody here knows me," she said with a sigh. "Who's going to call the cops?"

As if on cue, there was a loud knocking on the driver's side window. She looked up to see who was disturbing her and was met with the smiling face of Ray Best, the lone police officer of the incredibly small town of Oakville, Pennsylvania.

"Logan, are you still there?" Jack asked.

"You called the damn cops, didn't you?" she asked him, rolling down the window and forcing herself to smile at Ray. She heard Jack laughing as she placed the phone on the passenger seat and gave all her attention to the officer.

"Good morning, Logan," he said quietly as he removed his hat and took a look around the tranquil neighborhood. "Missy got a call about a suspicious looking person hanging around the place sitting in their car."

"You've got to be kidding me, Ray," she said. As much of a pain in the ass as Jack was, she knew he wouldn't have called the cops. Not now. Not while they were both going through one of the worst times of their lives. "I grew up in this town. Who here doesn't know me?"

"From what I understand, the Colliers' granddaughter arrived last night. She's moving in so she can give Peggy a hand with Henry's care," he said with a shrug and a slight nod toward the house. "Might've been her."

"Wonderful." Logan quickly brushed a hand over her face to wipe away any wetness. She pulled the key out of the ignition and began walking up the steps with Ray right behind her.

"Is there anything I can help you with?" he asked as she was unlocking the front door. She didn't answer right away, and he obviously took it as an invitation to keep talking. "I'm real sorry about your dad, Logan. If there's anything Missy and I can do to help you out, you just let us know, all right?"

"Thanks, Ray." Feeling like a heel wasn't something she anticipated, given the situation, but she knew Ray and his wife had been friends with both of her parents, and they were probably feeling a little lost after her father's sudden death too. She reminded herself the whole town had lost him, not just her and Jack. With the door unlocked, she turned and hugged the man who had always been like an uncle to her. "Tell Missy I'll call if I need anything."

"I heard on the news this morning Jack's coming home. It'll be good to see him again."

"Yeah, it will," she said, remembering she'd left her cell phone in the car and hadn't even hung up with Jack properly. She walked back down the steps with Ray and they both stopped short when a sports car came barreling around the corner. She chuckled in spite of her melancholy mood. "Speak of the devil."

"Ray, you old dog," Jack said as he got out of the car and lifted the much smaller Ray off the ground in a bear hug.

The contrast between them was laughable, and Logan found herself smiling at them. Jack was a huge man at six-foot-four and two hundred eighty pounds. He had their mother's blond hair and ocean blue eyes. Ray, on the other hand, was about six inches shorter, and close to a hundred pounds lighter. Ray laughed when Jack put him back on his own two feet and reached up to slap him on the shoulder.

"How are things, Undertaker?" Ray asked. The nickname caused an unexpected hitch in Logan's breathing, and she left the two of them to catch up. She grabbed her phone from the car and headed back into the house. She looked over at the house attached to her father's when the curtains moved again, but she didn't stop walking.

Great, she thought before entering the house. *Just what I need—a nosy neighbor.*

Things would go a lot smoother if she didn't allow herself the luxury of thinking about what she was doing, so she went directly up the stairs to her father's bedroom and headed for the closet. Maybe after she picked out the suit for him to be buried in, she'd allow herself some time to grieve properly.

❖

"Logan!"

She took a deep breath and closed her eyes, smiling ruefully at the fact her brother was the same now as he'd been before she left for college. He'd never been able to simply enter a room. He always had to make sure *everyone* knew he was there.

"I'm in the kitchen." A moment later, he walked in and sat at the table with her. He looked tired. She wondered if it had more to do with their father's death, or with the injuries he'd suffered in the current season. She'd followed his career closely, as had the rest of the town, and she knew he was more worried about his future in the NFL than he was letting on to the media.

"How are you?" he asked quietly.

"Just peachy, thanks for asking," she answered sarcastically. She immediately felt bad for the flippant tone. Her fingers traced the letters carved into the wooden kitchen table. *J.S.+ S.M. 4ever.* She felt tears welling up again but refused to let them fall. She remembered her father giving the table to her mother for her thirtieth birthday. The diner in town was remodeling and getting rid of all the tables and chairs. This particular table was the one her parents, John Swift and Susan Martin, had been sitting at the night he'd proposed to her. "I'm sorry, Jack. I'm just having a really hard time dealing with this."

"I understand, trust me," he said, his voice choked. He took in a deep breath as he looked around the kitchen, a slight smile tugging at his lips. After a moment he met Logan's eyes again. "You remember the time we tried to make cookies for Dad's birthday?"

"Jesus, Jack, don't remind me." She chuckled, and the realization dawned on her it was going to be good to have him around, for however long he was able to stay. Even though they were three years apart in age, they'd been inseparable until Jack started high school and decided it wasn't cool to hang out with his big sister anymore.

The birthday in question had been when Logan was twelve and Jack nine. As a surprise for their father, they'd decided to make his favorite sugar cookies. She remembered thinking the shortening looked and smelled a little bit funny, but at the time didn't worry too much about it. They found out later it hadn't really been shortening at all.

"Who the hell keeps old bacon grease in a Crisco can, and in the same cupboard where they actually keep the Crisco, no less?"

"He ate them though, didn't he?" Jack laughed.

"Every last one of them." Picturing him with a big smile on his face as the first bite went into his mouth was a memory worth cherishing. "You know, I haven't cooked since then, so if you're expecting home cooked meals while you're in town, you'll have to look elsewhere."

"I thought you'd have found a woman to do those things for you by now," Jack said.

"Please." She snorted. "In this town? I'm lucky the people here accept the fact I'm a lesbian. If I actually had a lover, some of them might not be so compliant. It's one thing to acknowledge it in the abstract, but if it's something you have to actually *see* every day, it can be a little too much for some people to deal with."

"Are you serious, Logan?" Jack went to the refrigerator where he found beers for them both. Logan took the one he held out to her even though it was only a little after noon. Who would blame her for indulging a little given the circumstances? She twisted the cap off and tossed it into the trash can behind her, listening when he continued. "The people in this town love you. I seem to remember Logan Swift could do no wrong."

"Then maybe I'm just uncomfortable with the thought I might be shoving it in people's collective faces," she said, irritated.

"I'm not trying to start a fight with you, all right?" Jack said with a shrug. "That's the last thing I want to do right now."

Logan felt like a heel—again. She stood and motioned for Jack to stand too. She put her arms around his neck, and his went around her waist. They stood like that for the longest time, just holding each other. Logan felt hot tears run down her cheeks and she buried her face in his shoulder. She realized it was the first time since she'd gotten the call about her father's fatal heart attack just over twenty-four hours earlier she'd allowed herself the luxury of breaking down.

CHAPTER TWO

There's no need to spy on them, dear."

Brooke Collier turned away from the window and faced her grandmother, Peggy. Not for the first time, she cursed her father for keeping these amazing people away from her for the first eighteen years of her life. She couldn't help feeling robbed of what probably would have been a wonderful childhood with her grandparents in her life. She considered herself lucky that since she'd turned eighteen, her father couldn't do a thing about denying her the right to see them. Now at the age of thirty-four, she had an incredible relationship with them, and was even closer to them than she was her father, which really wasn't too hard to accomplish since he'd rather spend time with a bottle than with her.

"I'm not spying, Gram." Brooke lied to her. "But I really think I should go and apologize to her."

"Whatever for?" her grandfather asked from his place in front of the television. He'd never missed an episode of *The Price is Right* since he'd retired from his job as an auto mechanic ten years earlier. Brooke smiled at the fact he never even glanced away from the television while they were talking.

Her heart ached when she thought about the reason she'd moved to Oakville. Her grandfather, Henry, had been diagnosed with Amyotrophic Lateral Sclerosis, which he preferred to call Lou Gehrig's Disease since Lou Gehrig had been his favorite baseball player of all time. He'd been confined to the wheelchair for the past year and a half, and it had been getting to be too much for her grandmother to take care of him on her own. It made sense for Brooke, a registered nurse, to come and help out. His speech hadn't yet been affected by the disease, but his legs were useless, as was his left arm.

"I didn't know who she was," Brooke said quietly. Watching the beautiful woman with the shoulder length black hair walk up the steps to the house attached to her grandparents' house had been interesting, to say the least. The woman had somehow managed to stir feelings in Brooke she thought were nonexistent since the horrible breakup with her last girlfriend not quite nine months earlier.

"What on earth are you talking about, Brooke?" her grandfather asked. There was a commercial on now, so he took the time to look at her as he asked the question.

"She was sitting out there in her car just staring up at the house," Brooke said as a way of explanation. "I thought she looked suspicious, so I called the police."

"Oh, for heaven's sake," her grandmother said. She walked to the front door, motioning for her grandfather to follow. "Henry, come on, we have to go apologize to Logan. She has enough to worry about with her father passing away."

"I'm not going anywhere," her grandfather grumbled, turning his attention back to the television. "Drew Carey sure as hell ain't Bob Barker, but damn it, I still love this show. You go on without me. I can talk to her later."

Brooke smiled with true affection before following her grandmother outside. She held a hand out to her grandmother in order to help her down the stairs, but her grandmother shook her head and pointed to the railing that separated the two front porches.

"I'll wait right here, dear. You'll get there a lot quicker if you just go over." She sat on the glider they'd had on the front porch for as long as Brooke had known them, and waited, her hands folded neatly in her lap.

Brooke did as she was told and stepped over the railing. She'd been surprised to learn of John Swift's death when her grandmother told her about it the night before. She took a deep breath before ringing the doorbell. A few moments passed with no noise coming from inside the house. She turned to her grandmother and shrugged.

"Maybe they left again," Brooke said even though she knew the car the woman had arrived in was still parked at the curb. The sports car the man had gotten out of was still there too. Brooke assumed the man was Jack, Logan's brother.

"They're still here," her grandmother said. "Sometimes the bell doesn't work. Maybe you should try knocking."

Brooke did, even though she'd heard the bell herself. Nevertheless, a few seconds after knocking, the door swung open, and she found herself face-to-face—or rather, face-to-shoulder—with the woman she'd been mentally drooling over just a few short minutes before.

"Yes?" the woman asked, sounding a bit agitated. She gave Brooke a thorough once-over with her eyes, and Brooke fidgeted uncomfortably under the scrutiny. "Can I help you?"

Brooke couldn't seem to make her mouth work, and why in the world was it so dry suddenly? She cleared her throat to try again, but the woman in the doorway was obviously impatient. And tall. Christ, she was tall. Brooke had never considered herself to be short at five foot ten, but this woman was a good four inches taller than she was. Brooke found herself standing up straighter in a feeble attempt to appear taller than she really was.

"Whatever you're selling, I'm not interested."

"Logan Swift, where are your manners?" Brooke's grandmother asked from her place on the porch, her voice raised.

Logan stopped her move to shut the door in Brooke's face and looked skyward before she plastered on a clearly fake smile. She sighed quietly before she stepped out on the porch.

"Please, forgive me, Peggy," Logan said before stepping over the railing. She leaned down to place a kiss on her grandmother's cheek and then took a seat next to her. Brooke watched the interaction with curiosity, and when Logan met her eyes, her breath caught in her throat. "You should have just told me you were here with Mrs. Collier."

The admonishment caught Brooke off guard, and she shrugged self-consciously. She was about to move to the other side of the porch herself when she was surprised by the giant—the *second* giant. Even though they were as different as night and day, there was no mistaking these two were related. He was blond while her hair was almost black, and his eyes were the strangest color blue, while hers were a piercing green. But strangely enough, they both resembled their father, and their status as giants convinced Brooke they were siblings.

"Logan, who is it?" He walked out the front door and his gaze lit on Brooke for a mere fraction of a second before his attention was drawn to the other people there. His face lit up and he didn't hesitate as he made his way over the railing. He crouched down in front of Brooke's grandmother and wrapped her small hands in his incredibly large ones. "Peggy Collier, how is the most beautiful woman in all of Oakville?"

Brooke watched in amazement as her grandmother blushed and swatted playfully at his arm. She wouldn't have thought she *could* blush, but apparently all it took was a little attention from a handsome and charming young man.

"I was so very sorry to hear about your father," her grandmother said as she extricated one of her hands from Jack's grip and took hold of Logan's hand. She shook her head. "It's such a shame. He was far too young to die."

Logan pulled away slowly and went back into the house without a word, her gaze slowly appraising Brooke's body once again on her way past. Brooke felt a fire begin deep in the pit of her belly and forced herself to look away. When she glanced back to the other side of the porch, Jack was watching her with a slight grin on his face. He began talking to her grandmother again, and Brooke decided to leave them to chat and go look for Logan. She'd never met John Swift's children, but he'd talked about them—a lot. He'd been very proud of them both.

Brooke walked past the stairway which went straight up from the small foyer. The house was a mirror opposite of her grandparent's house, which meant the kitchen was straight through the living room and dining room. She assumed the kitchen was where Logan had gone since she couldn't hear any footsteps coming from above. The hardwood floors were nicer in this house than the ones next door. She'd have to talk to her grandparents about getting theirs refinished.

"Are you all right?" Brooke asked softly when she found Logan in the kitchen, leaning over the sink, her shoulders shaking slightly. Brooke took a step backward when Logan straightened quickly and turned to glare at her.

"Do you make a habit of just walking into houses without an invitation?" she asked as she wiped away the tears on her cheeks.

Brooke was willing to give Logan the benefit of the doubt because she'd just suffered the loss of a loved one, but she hoped to God angry and rude weren't Logan's usual moods.

"I'm sorry. I only wanted to apologize to you." Brooke was struck again by Logan's looks and her height. Usually, she wouldn't even look twice at a woman whose demeanor was so rough, but there was something about her Brooke couldn't explain.

"You came in so you could apologize for coming in without an invitation?" Logan asked, looking and sounding as perplexed as Brooke felt at the question.

"No, Logan—"

"What makes you think it would be okay to walk in here uninvited?" Logan asked. She turned away again to stare out the window above the sink. "I don't even know you, so what in the world could you possibly have to apologize for?"

Brooke leaned against the doorframe and watched her in silence, trying hard to remember Logan was grieving, yet she found herself wondering why she would ever want to apologize to her for anything. Brooke wasn't sure what to say to her, because it seemed like anything she uttered set Logan off.

"My name is Brooke Collier," she said after a few moments of looking at Logan's backside. There was no denying it was a nice backside, but the personality attached to it left a lot to be desired. "I'm going to be living with my grandparents for a while. I'm really sorry to hear about your father's death. He was a good man."

"You knew him?"

"I'd spoken to him a few times, yes. He talked a lot about you and your brother." Brooke was feeling more and more uncomfortable the longer Logan stared out the window. Perhaps it was time to leave her alone with her thoughts. "Anyway, if you ever feel like you need a friend to talk to, I'm right next door."

"I'm sorry, but I'm really not in a very friendly mood right now," Logan said, turning to face her again. The biting tone was gone from her voice, and now she simply looked incredibly sad. The expression made Brooke's heart ache for her. "I have to bury my father the day after tomorrow. Maybe we could try again in a few days."

Brooke gave a curt nod and turned to leave, but then changed her mind. Both of Brooke's parents were still alive, so she really had no idea what Logan was going through.

"Please let me know if there's anything we can do for you, all right?" Brooke said. Logan nodded and Brooke decided it might be best to leave after all. No, she couldn't imagine what it would be like to lose either of her parents, but Brooke was fairly certain she wouldn't want a stranger trying to engage her in meaningless conversation.

"What did you come to apologize for?" Logan asked before she'd even taken two steps toward the front door.

"I'm the one who called the police," Brooke said, feeling her cheeks flush as she turned back to face Logan. "I'm sorry, but I didn't know who you were, and you were just sitting out there staring at the house."

"It's okay." Logan looked like she was trying not to laugh. "I'd rather you call the cops than come outside with your granddad's shotgun."

"He has one?" Brooke asked. He was in the early stages of Alzheimer's on top of the ALS, and she shuddered to think what might happen. Of course the ALS would probably prevent him from using the gun, but it was still an alarming thought.

"More than one. He used to be an avid hunter. He and my father used to go out whenever they got the chance, which was usually every weekend." Logan must have seen the concern on her face because she shook her head. "Don't worry. Peggy has them all locked away where he can't get to them."

"Of course." Brooke quickly turned to go, leaving Logan staring after her. She didn't want anyone, especially a stranger, to see the panic she was sure was written all over her face.

CHAPTER THREE

"D amn, Logan," Jack said when he came back into the kitchen. "You should have seen the way she was looking at you, sis."

"What the hell are you talking about?"

"Brooke. She was eyeing you like you were spread out on a buffet table." He laughed. "Or maybe she was just wishing you were."

"You are so full of shit," Logan said as she sat at the table again. She took a drink of her beer and studied his face to see if he was lying. When they were growing up, their mother always said she could tell when Jack was lying by the little twitch he got under his left eye. That and the fact he couldn't look you in the eye when he was lying. Now, he was sustaining eye contact *and* there was no visible twitch. Maybe he'd gotten better at lying, although, Logan could have sworn she almost felt Brooke's eyes on her ass earlier while she was standing at the sink, but—no. "You're full of shit."

"Whatever." Jack shook his head and took a drink of his beer.

"Do you remember ever hearing the Colliers had another child? Brooke must be my age, and Marlene isn't quite fifty yet, so I'm pretty sure she isn't her mother."

"Maybe she is Brooke's mother and that's why we never heard about Brooke before." Jack shrugged. "Marlene could have been about sixteen when she was born."

"I don't know," Logan said. "Maybe. But we would've noticed if there had been a kid in the house next door, don't you think?"

"Or maybe there's a long-lost child they don't ever talk about, and Brooke is the child of the devil." Jack made spooky sounds and weird gestures with his hands.

"When do you have to get back to Cleveland?" Logan rolled her eyes at him before changing the subject. Jack only looked away from her and didn't answer. "Jack? What aren't you telling me, little bro?"

Logan watched as he took a deep breath and began peeling little pieces of the label off his beer bottle. Five minutes later, the label was in shreds on the table before him, and he still hadn't spoken. Logan sighed and leaned forward.

"I think you've forgotten I can be just as stubborn as you are. I'll sit here all night waiting for you to talk if that's what it takes," Logan said, even though they both knew it wasn't true. She had too much work to do before the funeral. Just thinking about it made her feel like someone took a fistful of her heart and squeezed. She tried to shove the thought from her mind. "It's worse than what they've been reporting, isn't it?"

"Yeah," he said, his voice quiet. He reminded Logan of the little boy he used to be—the one who'd come home after breaking a neighbor's window with a baseball, knowing he was going to be punished. After another moment or two, he finally met her eyes. "The last concussion was a grade four. They won't let me play until after I'm evaluated and cleared by a specialist in Pittsburgh. I have an appointment next week."

"So you're more than likely out for the season since there's only four games left." Logan had a sneaking suspicion they weren't talking just about the *current* season. This would be his fourth concussion in the past three years, and they both knew brain injuries weren't something to take lightly. When he didn't answer her question, she felt her heart rate speed up. Jesus, wasn't it enough they'd just lost their father? "Your career might be over. That's what you're trying not to say, isn't it, Jack?"

"Washed up at the age of thirty. Five years from now nobody will even remember me."

"Not true." Logan went to kneel beside his chair. Tears ran down his cheeks, undermining the forced smile. "You've won two Super Bowls, went to three Pro Bowls, and you hold the records for most sacks in a single game *and* for a season. Those records won't be broken anytime soon. You didn't get the nickname *Undertaker* just because Dad was a funeral director. You earned it by crushing quarterbacks.

You're a star, Jack, and people will never forget you. You'll be in the Football Hall of Fame someday, trust me."

"You always were good for my ego," he said with a slight chuckle.

"And you for mine, bro. That's why I like having you around."

"When they told me, you know what my first thought was? My life will never be the same. How selfish is that? Because then I got the call from you yesterday afternoon about Dad. I don't even know up from down anymore, Logan. The possibility of my playing days being over is so insignificant compared to everything else in life. It's just a fucking game I was lucky enough to be paid to play, you know? I should have been here. I never should have gone away to play college ball. I should have gone to school to be a funeral director like Dad wanted me to."

"Hey, Jack, he was proud of you. Don't you ever doubt that. Man, you should have seen the way he would beam whenever someone would mention a sack you made in the last game. He never begrudged you following your dream."

"What about you?"

"What about me?"

"You wanted to be a doctor, Logan. You had to give up *your* dream when I got my full ride to Penn State."

"I didn't *have* to do anything, Jack. It was my choice to switch gears and take mortuary science instead of continuing with med school. Dad never asked me to do it. I think he was more surprised than anyone when I told him about it." Logan tried not to cry as she remembered the day she'd made the decision to change career paths. "And for the record, it wasn't when you got the scholarship. It was when Mom died. We all knew by then you'd have a career in football, and I knew Dad would be lost living here all on his own. I sat him down the day after Mom's funeral and told him about it.

"I've always believed things worked out the way they were supposed to for both of us, Jack." Logan stood and leaned against the kitchen counter, her arms folded across her chest. "I was so proud of all the recruiters going to see your high school games, the friends I had at college were sick of hearing about you. You're my little brother, Jack. There's nothing that'll ever change that. I love you, and if your career is over, we'll figure things out together if it's what you want."

"If? Don't you mean when?"

"*If* it's over now or *when* it's over six or eight years down the road, whatever." Logan shifted her weight from one foot to the other and waited for him to look at her. "You know I'll always be here for you."

"You're the only family I have left, Logan. I hope you know how much you mean to me."

Logan fought back tears. After struggling to not look away from him, she forced a smile.

"I've got work to do," she said as she pushed away from the counter and grabbed the coat she'd draped over the back of the chair.

"Logan?" He was looking down at his hands when she turned to look at him. "Are you really doing the embalming yourself? Why don't you have Ernie do it?"

"Why would I?"

"I just don't understand how you can do it. I mean, he's our father."

"Exactly. He's our father. How can I *not* do it?"

She really hoped he could appreciate her reasons for handling the embalming on her own. Their father had done it for their mother, and while she hadn't truly understood it then, she did now. It was her responsibility to take care of him, and there was no way in hell she was going to let anyone else do it. Especially someone from another funeral home in another town. She knew her father would never want that.

❖

Six hours later, her father lay on the table, a white sheet covering everything but his head, and Logan thought for a moment how he looked as if he were simply sleeping. He'd look even better after the makeup was applied. The embalming was done, she'd washed the body and styled his hair the way he'd had it for the past twenty years, and he was finally ready to be dressed. That part she would leave to her apprentice and makeup artist, Billy Best.

Ray and Missy had been less than thrilled when their only son made the decision to go into mortuary science, but the kid was good, and Logan and her father had been grateful to have him around. There wasn't a lot of need for their services in Oakville itself, but Swift Funeral Home had been around for over a hundred years, and they'd built a reputation good enough to bring in business from miles around.

"You ready for me yet?" Billy asked as he stuck his head in and looked at her.

"Yeah," she said. She removed her gown and gloves, which she tossed into the medical waste basket by the desk, then went to the sink to wash her hands as Billy grabbed the clothes she'd brought and started to dress him. Logan wanted to leave. She didn't think she could stand to watch Billy working on her father. She'd almost reached the door when Billy spoke again.

"How's…" He paused, and Logan turned to face him. "Who's the nurse in Erie you see once in a while?"

"Gretchen?" Logan asked. She'd often wondered if Billy was gay, but he'd never indicated one way or the other, and Logan didn't think it was her place to come right out and ask. He'd never mentioned a girlfriend—or a boyfriend, for that matter. But Logan thought his fascination with her private life was a bit strange.

"I don't know why I can never remember her name." He chuckled. "Have you seen her lately?"

"No, I haven't, Billy. She wanted more from me than I was willing to give, and I told her we couldn't see each other anymore."

Even though she didn't want to, she felt compelled to watch as Billy began dressing her father. She'd known Billy since they were kids, and he and Jack had been best friends for years. She knew this couldn't be easy for Billy either, but he had a way of being able to completely block out the person he was working on. Logan could usually do it too, but she hadn't been able to accomplish it this time.

"Are you ever going to settle down?" Billy asked, bringing her out of her thoughts. "You know your dad was always hoping you'd find a nice girl to spend your life with."

"Billy, I've seen way too much death in my lifetime. I've seen what it does to the people left behind—the heartache, the devastation, and the emptiness. I also saw it in my dad when my mother died. I don't ever want to experience a loss so all consuming. I'm quite content with my life exactly as it is."

Billy looked at her with an expression that told her he thought she was full of shit. It was the same way her father looked at her whenever they'd talk about her lack of a girlfriend. But she didn't care what anyone thought. It was her life, and after seeing how her mother's death came so close to completely destroying her father, she had no desire to ever live through something like it herself. Just the thought of it scared her senseless. What was the old saying?

It's better to have loved and lost than never to have loved at all. Bullshit.

Logan *never* wanted to fall in love, and she'd be perfectly happy to spend the rest of her life alone. That's exactly how she'd lived her life up to now, and how she'd continue to live it forevermore.

❖

It was almost seven when she got back to the house, and she was surprised to find Jack asleep on the couch, the TV blaring in front of him. She shook her head at the fast food bag on the floor, and the empty beer bottles on the coffee table. The Cleveland Browns were playing the Cincinnati Bengals on Thursday Night Football.

"Hey, sleepyhead." She pushed on his shoulder, and he opened one eye before covering his head and groaning.

"Leave me alone," he said, his voice nothing short of a whine. "I want to sleep until Christmas."

"Christmas is over a month away, dude."

He put his hands behind his head and smiled up at her.

"Did you really just call me *dude*?"

"I did." She laughed and picked up his trash to take it to the kitchen. "I guess I've been spending too much time with Billy."

"Billy Best?" Jack sat up quickly and winced. Logan dropped the bag and went to sit next to him on the couch.

"Are you all right?"

"I'm fine. I just shouldn't sit up so fast. My head doesn't seem to like sudden movements anymore." He opened one eye and glanced at the television before wincing again. "Fuck. They can't do shit without me in the lineup. The Browns will never make it to the Super Bowl again."

"This from the man who says no one will remember him in five years. Sounds like your ego is still very much intact."

"What can I say?"

Logan knew the impending news about his injury was bothering him way more than he'd ever admit. She worried he'd be lost if he couldn't play football, which had been his life for the past fifteen years. She eyed the six beer bottles on the coffee table in front of them.

"Are you supposed to be drinking this much?"

"Probably not, but you aren't my mother. I'm a grown man, Logan. I'll drink a beer or six if I want to."

"I don't want to have to bury you too, Jack." Logan fought the emotion welling up inside her at just the thought of it. Her breathing quickened, but she hoped it was the only outward sign of her distress at the visual her thought evoked. Her father's death had somehow turned her into an emotional ball of mush, and she didn't like it at all. The sooner she could get back to normal, everyday life the better.

"Not gonna happen, sis," he said with an affectionate smile. He draped an arm over her shoulders and hugged her close. "You're stuck with me for a lot of years yet."

"Good." She went to the kitchen, and when she came back with a beer, Jack wasn't on the couch anymore and the Browns were losing by two touchdowns with less than five minutes to play. She sighed and went out to the front porch. A pizza delivery car pulled up to the curb as she sat on one of the two chairs her father had put out there for them to sit in on warm summer nights. It was anything but warm now, being only a week away from Thanksgiving. The porch light next door went on as the pizza guy went up the walk.

"That'll be twenty-three dollars, ma'am," the driver said. Logan couldn't see whether it was Peggy or Brooke who was at the door, but she hoped it was Peggy. She really didn't want to have to make small talk with Brooke. For some reason, the woman made her nervous, and that was so not like her.

"Keep the change." Brooke's cheery voice sliced through the cool night air. "You can leave the sodas on the porch and I'll come right back for them."

"Thank you, ma'am," the young man said as he tipped his ball cap and returned to his car.

Logan contemplated going back inside, but just as Brooke was coming back for the sodas, Jack emerged from the house.

"Good evening," he said to Brooke, who jumped as if she'd been electrocuted.

"Jesus, you scared the hell out of me."

"Why?" Logan said. "You can't see his face without *our* porch light on."

"Bitch," Jack said with a laugh.

"Bastard."

"Do you two always call each other names?"

"I take it you don't have any siblings." After flipping on their porch light, Jack sat in the chair next to Logan and put his feet up on the railing in front of him. "Which of course is my way of saying yes, we do always call each other names."

"No, I'm an only child." Brooke glanced back through the storm door into the house and then back at Logan and Jack. "Listen, I ordered a pizza because my grandfather insisted on it for dinner, but now he's fallen asleep and Gram doesn't want to wake him. There's more than enough for the two of us, so if you'd like some, you're welcome to come over and join us."

"Don't make that offer to him," Logan said seriously. "He'll eat the whole damn thing. He thinks he's still a growing boy."

"How about you bring us the leftovers when you're done eating?" Jack suggested. Logan tried not to smile at the way he ignored her jab.

"You got it." She met Logan's eyes, but Logan looked away quickly before taking a long drink of her beer.

"You have got to be the densest person I've ever known," Jack said when Brooke had disappeared inside the house.

"What the hell are you talking about?"

"I'm talking about you and your fight or flight mentality. That woman wants you, and you're going to do everything in your power to ignore the signs."

"In case you've forgotten, I just met her for the first time this afternoon."

"Yeah, and when Christmas gets here you'll still be doing all you can to stay away from her, won't you?" Jack shook his head. "Just stop trying to avoid relationships, Logan."

"Look who's talking," Logan said quietly. "The man who's never had a relationship last more than a couple of months."

"Which is a couple of months longer than you've ever had, if I'm not mistaken. I'm not here to argue with you, all right? I know why you avoid commitment, I really do. I'm just trying to say you might be missing out on something pretty damn great because you're afraid of losing someone. Just think about it, Logan."

She stayed silent as he got up and went back inside the house. Who the hell did he think he was? He didn't know anything about her or her reasons for wanting to be alone. If he'd seen how utterly devastated their father had been after their mother's death, maybe he could understand it, but he'd been fifteen and a self-involved teenager at the time. He'd only been able to see his own grief and nobody else's mattered to him. She took a deep breath and closed her eyes. Living alone wasn't so bad if you didn't think about what you might be missing.

CHAPTER FOUR

T he viewing is tonight then?" Brooke's grandmother asked when Logan came by the next morning to tell them what time the funeral would be.

"Yes, from seven till nine. The funeral will be tomorrow morning at eleven."

Brooke could see the pain in Logan's eyes and wondered what it cost her to hold her emotions in. It certainly couldn't be healthy. She found herself wishing Logan would let her in enough to help her through it all. But she knew from conversations with John, his daughter would never let anyone close enough to see her anguish.

"We'll be there," her grandmother said. "Is there anything you or Jack need? You know we'll help out any way we can, dear."

"Thank you, but I think we have everything under control, Peggy," Logan said. She smiled, but to Brooke it looked like an attempt to cover her pain.

"Is that Logan Swift's voice I hear?" Brooke's grandfather called from down the hall. "Somebody come help me with this blasted wheelchair!"

Brooke excused herself to go and help him. Logan's eyes met hers and Brooke swore she could feel a jolt of electricity between them. But that was crazy, she thought to herself as she tore her gaze away from Logan. What the hell was going on here? Brooke wasn't the type to fall for the first good-looking woman she came across. And besides, she'd promised herself she wouldn't get involved with anyone ever again after what Wendy had done to her. She was beginning to understand the instant attraction to Logan might make that promise harder to keep than she'd thought.

She hurried down the hallway and helped her grandfather maneuver the chair through the doorway and watched in amused silence as he sped away from her once he was through. If the ALS robbed him of the use of his right hand and arm, he'd never be able to get around on his own. Brooke was worried about how it would crush him, because he was a proud man. It was one thing to need help getting in and out of the chair and the bed, but quite another to rely on someone else for absolutely everything. She couldn't imagine what that would feel like.

"Have a seat, Logan. I need to talk to you about something," he said. Brooke watched in silence and took a seat next to her grandmother. Logan sat on the couch.

"What's up, Henry?" Logan asked while he moved his chair so he was in front of her.

"I'm really sorry about your dad. John was a good man, and he and your mother raised a couple of wonderful kids. You and Jack are like our own grandchildren, but I guess I really don't need to tell you that do I? If there's ever anything either of you need, all you have to do is ask, all right?"

Logan didn't answer right away and Brooke saw her eyes tearing up when she glanced away. She looked so lost. Brooke had the urge to hold her and assure her everything would be okay, even though there was no possible way she could make the promise.

"Thank you, Henry," Logan finally said, her voice strained. "I appreciate it. I really should be getting back home. We'll see you tonight at the viewing."

"Hold on there, dear," her grandfather said, placing a hand on her knee, which stopped her from standing. "I need to discuss a little business with you."

"Come, Brooke," her grandmother said quietly. "Let's leave them alone to discuss their business."

Brooke did as she was told, but when she turned back to look into the living room, she saw her grandfather handing Logan an envelope overstuffed with papers.

"What's going on, Gram?"

"I don't know what you mean, dear," her grandmother said. Brooke watched in silence as her grandmother moved around the kitchen, obviously only pretending to be busy because all she was really doing was rearranging things.

"What business does he have with Logan?"

"I'm sure I don't know."

"Then why did you rush me out of the room?"

Her grandmother stopped and stared out the window. Brooke noticed how her body shook slightly. Her grandmother looked so frail standing there in spite of the fact she was an active, strong woman. She had balked at the idea of Brooke moving in to help her take care of her husband, but Brooke's aunt Marlene had made her see the practicality of it. Brooke walked up behind her and placed a gentle hand on her grandmother's shoulder.

"Please, Gram, I'm not a child."

"No, I suppose you're right," her grandmother finally said. "John Swift owned the funeral home in town. You know that, right?"

"Of course." Brooke kept her voice as soft as she could. She had the feeling if she didn't it might break the spell and her grandmother would stop talking.

"Logan worked with him. I would imagine she'll be taking over the business now. It's been in their family for more than a century."

Brooke's throat tightened as the words sank in. There was only one reason she could think of for an ill, elderly man to have business with an undertaker.

"He's pre-planning his funeral?" Brooke managed to ask even though she was having trouble breathing. Her grandmother simply nodded, and Brooke swallowed hard. "Is he dying, Gram? Is there something you haven't told me?"

Brooke knew it was a ridiculous question because ALS was incurable. Apparently her mind wasn't quite ready to deal with the fact concerning her own grandfather. Thankfully her grandmother seemed to know what she meant and didn't take the question as though it was asked by someone who didn't know the severity of his illness.

"Good heavens, no, child," she said, turning to face Brooke. Her smile helped to ease Brooke's panic. "But then again, we're all dying, aren't we? After all, no one expected John Swift to be dead at fifty-five. Your grandfather spoke with him about this a couple years ago. I'd imagine he just wants to make sure Logan's up to speed on everything they'd talked about."

"You're sure you aren't keeping anything from me?"

"Brooke, honey, you know better than I do the ALS is going to take him one day. My hope is it won't be anytime soon, but we never know what tomorrow's going to bring, do we? He wants to deal with it all now, so I won't have to worry about it if his time comes before mine."

Brooke stared at her grandmother in disbelief. How could she speak of death in such a nonchalant way? Brooke worked in the medical profession and could never be so casual about it. As a nurse she'd seen her share of unexpected death and knew it could happen at any time—and to anyone—regardless of age or health. She couldn't imagine speaking of a spouse's death in such a detached way, though.

She looked back out to the living room and saw Logan standing and nodding as her grandfather spoke to her. As Logan turned to leave, she hesitated and placed a hand on his shoulder for a moment before walking out the door.

She'd only known these wonderful people for less than half her life, but Brooke couldn't bear the thought of either of them dying so soon. She knew they were well into their seventies, and as her grandmother had said, her grandfather's ALS would eventually take his life. The rational part of her brain reminded her most people died within five years of their diagnosis. Brooke hoped against hope he might be one of the few who lived longer. He'd been diagnosed three years earlier, so she knew the odds of him living more than another year or two were slim. She held back her tears and headed out the door after Logan.

Logan shoved the overstuffed envelope into her jacket pocket as she pulled the door closed behind her. Her father had started working with the Colliers on their pre-arranged funerals a few years earlier, and she knew it was what they wanted, but it didn't mean she liked it. Pre-arranged funerals were ill-advised as far as she was concerned.

Having people spend their time and money planning for their deaths simply never made sense to her. Yes, death was an inevitable part of life but why not enjoy life while you're still able to? Most of the time people would pick out their casket in advance, but then when the time came the casket they wanted and had already paid for simply wasn't being made any longer. Then the survivors still had to get involved, which was exactly what the deceased had wanted to avoid by planning for everything in advance. But, it was a service they provided, and she would never deny anyone if it was what they truly wanted to do.

She took a deep breath and went back to her own side of the porch when she heard the Colliers' door open. She turned just as Brooke came running out.

"What the hell?" Brooke slammed the door behind her and walked closer to Logan. Logan took an involuntary step back at the fury she saw in Brooke's deep blue eyes. The fact they were on opposite sides of the railing seemed to make no difference. "You didn't tell me you bury people for a living."

"Excuse me?"

Logan watched as Brooke paced and ran a hand through her short brown hair. She knew this wasn't the time to be checking out the new neighbor, but damn it, she couldn't help herself. Brooke was beautiful, and even more so when she was angry, apparently. After a moment, Brooke stopped fuming and stood still. She wrapped her arms around herself as though finally realizing it was only twenty degrees outside. Without thinking, Logan removed her own jacket and went back to the other side of the porch in order to put it around Brooke's shoulders.

"Don't touch me," Brooke said, sounding like she wanted to be mad but wasn't quite pulling it off. She allowed Logan to put the jacket on her but then stepped away quickly. "Why didn't you tell me?"

"In case you've forgotten, I only just met you yesterday. It isn't usually something I tell people the moment I meet them." Logan sat on the glider and leaned forward, her elbows resting on her knees. "For some reason, it tends to make most people a bit uncomfortable. But while we're on the subject, I don't believe you told me what you do for a living either."

"I'm a nurse." Brooke sighed as if admitting defeat and took a seat next to her. Logan sat back and waited for her to continue. "I left my job at Temple Hospital's ER in Philadelphia to come up here so I could help her take care of him."

"That must have been a difficult decision to make. You had to be earning a good living there, and now you're here making nothing."

"It wasn't nearly as difficult as you might think." Brooke let out a short, humorless bark of laughter. "There was absolutely nothing to keep me there any longer. I had a few friends of course, but I lost most of them when my relationship blew up in my face. It sucks how people always seem to take sides when breakups happen, isn't it?"

Logan didn't know how to answer because she'd always avoided relationships. Except for Julie, who seemed like a lifetime ago. Twenty-one-years old *was* a lifetime ago as far as she was concerned. She looked into Brooke's expressive blue eyes.

"I've heard things can happen that way sometimes, but thankfully, I've never had the experience."

"What?" Brooke seemed genuinely surprised. She pulled Logan's jacket tighter around her shoulders and shivered. "You've never lost friends in a breakup?"

"I've only ever had one breakup, and none of our friends knew we were in a relationship to begin with. It was in college and she didn't want anyone to know she was a lesbian."

Logan waited for the admonishment she was sure would come whenever she outed herself to someone new, but she was surprised when whatever anger was left in Brooke's eyes softened.

"Women suck, don't they?" Brooke said after a moment. Logan smiled and finally began to relax a bit. "They have the ability to fuck up your life with nothing more than a few words."

"Only if you let them."

"You don't?"

"Not if I can help it," Logan said with a grin. "I don't let anyone close enough to be able to mess with my life. Short and casual is how I like my relationships. Nobody gets hurt if you both know the ground rules up front, right?"

"I wish I'd had the foresight to be casual with Wendy. I swear to God that relationship almost killed me."

"Hey, Logan, we should get going if we want to get there before people start showing up," Jack said as he came out on the porch. His step faltered when he saw the two of them sitting together, Brooke with Logan's jacket around her shoulders. "I knew it."

"You don't know shit, Jack," Logan said. "This isn't what you think so get your mind out of the gutter."

"Then what is it?"

"Two people talking. It's nothing more than a couple of new friends getting to know each other a little better." Logan stood and looked down at Brooke and lowered her voice so Jack couldn't overhear. "Do you think we could maybe continue this later? It's really nice being able to talk to someone about these things."

"Anytime," Brooke said. She stood and started to shrug the jacket off her shoulders but Logan stopped her.

"Keep it. You can always give it back to me tonight if you go to the viewing with your grandparents. If not, I know where you live."

"I'll see you later then." Brooke smiled at both of them before disappearing back into the house.

Logan avoided her brother's amused look as she shouldered past him into their own house. She ignored his laughter and went about getting her clothes ready for the viewing.

CHAPTER FIVE

Logan stood stiffly in the back of the room with Jack by her side. She honestly didn't think she'd make it through the viewing if he weren't there. They were both dressed in black suits, hers just a touch more feminine because her white shirt was open at the throat. His tie looked as though it was choking him.

She thought of the bottle of tequila upstairs in her kitchen. If she was quick, she could probably get a couple of shots down before anybody even knew she'd left. No, she told herself. Drinking at work was a definite no-no.

"Have you finished writing the eulogy yet?" Logan asked without taking her eyes from the casket in the front of the room.

"I thought you were going to take care of it," Jack said when she shot him a look of panic. "Relax, it's done. Although I'm not sure why you want me to deliver it."

"You're a better public speaker than I am," she said, barely resisting the urge to slug him in the arm for scaring the hell out of her.

The evening dragged on while all of their father's friends and acquaintances stopped by to pay their respects. Logan found herself surprised by how many people were in attendance. She knew he'd been loved and respected by many, but seeing just how many caused a lump in her throat she was finding difficult to dislodge.

People were crying, and Jack seemed to know how it was affecting her. Every time she thought she was going to lose it, his hand would grasp hers tightly and she'd calm down again. When Ray and Missy Best walked in, Logan wondered briefly who was on duty protecting the town, but then she realized the entire town was in their funeral home at the moment. She closed her eyes and fought back tears for what seemed like the hundredth time. Jack's arm went around her shoulders.

"You *can* cry, you know," he said quietly, his mouth close to her ear. "It's a normal part of grieving. How many times did we hear Dad say that to people?"

"Thousands." She knew it was true, but it didn't make it any easier. She'd cried uncontrollably at her mother's funeral when she'd only been eighteen. Logan hadn't fully understood then she was supposed to help people through their grief, and it felt somehow wrong for her to give in to her own now. Her father had never cried during her mother's funeral. He'd never cried in front of anyone, as far as Logan knew. But she heard him at night, when he thought he was alone, crying like a baby. It had nearly killed her inside to know he was suffering alone, but Logan knew he would never give in to his grief in front of her, so she'd never said anything to him about it. "Maybe tens of thousands."

She pulled away and saw the tears running down Jack's cheeks. It undid her, and she threw her arms around his neck and sobbed into his shoulder. He held her tightly and they cried together for their father, as they'd done for their mother fifteen years before.

"I wish there was something we could do for them," Brooke said when she saw Logan and Jack in the back of the room. It seemed as if everyone saw them, but no one went to comfort them. She took a step in their direction, but her grandmother placed a hand on her arm, effectively stopping her.

"Let them be, dear," she said quietly. "The life of a funeral director is a lonely job. John once said to us it didn't matter how many friends he had, no one ever really wanted to be very close to him. There's a stigma attached to the profession, and they know it. They'll be fine."

Brooke stood in shock staring at her grandmother. Had she really spoken those words? She shook her head in disbelief.

"You've both said Logan and Jack are like your own grand-children. How can you possibly feel that way and still say what you just said?"

"Because it's true, Brooke," her grandfather said. "They *are* like our own family. They know how we feel about them, and they know if they need anything, we'll do what we can to help. But we won't force ourselves into their mourning. John Swift was a good man, and it's a damn shame he had to die so young. Like your grandmother and me, there are some people in the world who can look past the profession. I hope you'll be one of them. I think Logan could really use a friend her own age. But as far as grieving, that isn't something you can help them with. They'll pull each other through it."

"Of course." As long as Logan allowed her to be a friend, she thought. Their conversation earlier in the day had been promising. It had been a little scary how easy she was to talk to. She hadn't talked with anyone other than Aunt Marlene about what had happened between her and Wendy before. It would definitely be good to have a friend.

Brooke had just sat down with a cup of hot chocolate when she heard Logan and Jack coming home. Her grandparents had been asleep for over an hour so she decided it would be all right if she went next door for a few minutes. Given how easy it was to hear the Swifts moving around in their half of the house, she knew she'd be able to hear her grandparents if they decided to get up and needed her for anything.

"Hey," Logan said with a weary smile as she opened the door. She stepped aside and motioned for Brooke to enter.

"I hope it's okay to come over so late," Brooke said as she handed over the jacket Logan had loaned her earlier. She held a hand up to acknowledge Jack sitting on the couch. He waved back and stood with a yawn.

"I'm going to go on up to bed, sis," he said with an exaggerated wink. "Don't do anything I wouldn't do."

"Bastard," Logan muttered under her breath. She led Brooke into the kitchen and offered her something to drink. "Don't pay any attention to him. He thinks he's funny. I guess I have only myself to blame though because I always laughed at his stupid jokes when we were growing up."

"Well, given the fact he's good-looking *and* a famous football player, I'd think there isn't much he wouldn't do, so that wouldn't really limit us, would it?" Brooke felt her face flush when Logan stared at her, one eyebrow raised in question. God, she hoped that didn't sound like a come-on line. Or maybe she hoped it did. She was so confused she didn't know what she wanted anymore.

"Are you a football fan?" Logan finally asked as she turned away to make coffee.

"Eagles. I grew up in Philadelphia."

"Right. We don't much care for the Eagles on this side of the state. We're almost exactly halfway between Pittsburgh and Buffalo, so growing up we had some pretty heated rivalries in this house. Jack and I rooted for the Bills, and our parents were Steelers fans all the way."

"And now?"

"Well, I kind of *have* to root for the Browns, you know, since Jack is their superstar defensive player, but my heart will always be with the Bills. And let me tell you, it's been a bit painful over the years." Logan finished up with the coffee maker and took a seat across from Brooke. She looked uncomfortable, and Brooke wondered why. "So how come I've never seen you around here before? I've known Henry and Peggy all my life."

"I guess you were never around when I came to visit," Brooke said with a shrug. "I've been here for Thanksgiving and Christmas every year since I turned eighteen."

"Why since you turned eighteen? Why not before?"

"My father wouldn't allow me to visit. I never met them until I was eighteen and Aunt Marlene urged me to come here."

"I know Marlene. She's a really great person. She and her son Shane come to visit every summer." Logan held their eye contact a little too long, but Brooke refused to look away. Logan finally did after a few moments, and Brooke relaxed. "Why wouldn't your dad let you visit? You know, come to think of it, I'm not sure I ever remember anyone mentioning the Colliers having had a son. There definitely wasn't one around since I've known them."

"I don't think they lived here when he was growing up. And as far as him not allowing me to visit, he always told me they were dead." It had been a constant source of friction between her and her parents since Marlene had managed to introduce her to her grandparents, but no one would ever explain to her why her father and his parents were estranged. "I figured it must be something pretty serious since he never talked about them, and they've never mentioned him in conversations with me. I can't seem to get up the nerve to ask Gram about it either."

Logan nodded as though she completely understood the situation, but how could she? Of course, being a funeral director, perhaps Logan had a better knowledge of family dynamics than Brooke could ever hope to have. Maybe she really did understand the situation. Or maybe she was simply being polite by nodding in what she felt were the right places. Nevertheless, Brooke was relieved when Logan changed the subject.

"Maybe it's none of my business, but you said earlier your last relationship almost killed you." Logan stood to get them each a cup of the coffee. "Do you want to talk about it?"

"There's nothing really to talk about. I was stupid enough to think things were going great between us. We were both working swing shift at the time. I came home from work around one in the morning, and she was gone." Brooke took a sip of the coffee Logan handed her, hoping the warmth of it would chase away the chill she felt. She glanced at Logan when she took her seat again and wondered what about her could make it so easy to tell her these things. She took a deep breath as Logan simply watched her in silence, waiting for her to continue. "She'd left me a note on the coffee table saying she'd moved out. She took all her things but left me the television and DVR, which she made sound like she was doing me a favor even though I was the one who paid for them in the first place."

"What was her reason for leaving?"

"She said she didn't love me, and apparently, she never did. I guess she figured it would be easier to have some friends come and move her out when she knew I wasn't going to be home than to be forced to tell me those things to my face. She moved in with a couple she knew from where she worked. I didn't know it at the time, but they were all sleeping together."

"Ouch." Logan winced but said nothing more.

Brooke appreciated the fact Logan was letting her tell the story on her own terms and not asking a ton of questions. What she had to say next was the hardest. It had humiliated her at the time, but almost a year removed from the situation, she was simply angry to realize she'd allowed Wendy to manipulate her so thoroughly.

"A married couple. A *straight* married couple. I guess Wendy wanted a child, which was news to me. Of course, they were more than happy to accommodate her. I heard through the rumor mill she had the baby a couple months ago, but I haven't spoken with her since our relationship ended around nine months ago."

"Then she was sleeping with them before she left you."

"Yep. She was a master at the art of lying. I hate myself for letting her fool me for so long."

"Yet you still love her."

Brooke's first reaction was to scoff at Logan's statement. The past nine months ran through her mind in a matter of seconds. At first, she'd begged Wendy to come back to her. When she'd found out the true living arrangement she had chosen, Brooke was disgusted and then refused to take her calls when she would try getting in touch with her. When she finally found out Wendy was pregnant, Brooke washed her hands of the entire mess. Unfortunately, it hadn't been so easy to get her heart to believe she wanted nothing more to do with her. Was she still in love with her? No, she most definitely was not. But that didn't mean the wounds weren't still raw.

"It's okay if you are," Logan said with a slight shrug when Brooke didn't respond right away.

Brooke wanted to correct her assumption, but something held her back. What would be the point in either confirming or denying what she felt for her ex? The only reason she could think of would be if she were trying to pursue something with Logan. Sleeping with the next-door neighbor would definitely not be a good idea. Even if said neighbor *was* the most gorgeous woman Brooke had ever laid eyes on.

"So, what do you do for fun around here?" Brooke asked in a feeble attempt to get her mind off the track it was heading down. She dared to meet Logan's eyes and saw what she could only describe as amusement. Apparently, her change of subject hadn't been as inconspicuous as she'd hoped it would be.

"Around here? Not a hell of a lot. In case you hadn't noticed, Oakville is one of those places you'd miss if you blinked." Logan set her coffee cup down and scratched the back of her neck. "Erie's about forty minutes away, but if you're looking for the kind of fun you can only have with like-minded women, we're almost two hours from both Buffalo and Pittsburgh. There is a bar in Erie, but it's mostly men and not many women go there."

"And which do you prefer? Buffalo or Pittsburgh?"

"Buffalo. Up there you get more women who are vacationing since it's pretty close to both Niagara Falls and Canada."

"Less of a chance you'd ever run into them again?" Brooke regretted the comment as soon as the words left her mouth. Logan's body stiffened slightly and Brooke could almost hear the walls going up around her. "I'm sorry. I didn't mean anything by it."

"It's not a big deal. I don't need you or anyone else to approve of how I live my life."

Brooke watched in silence as Logan stood and dumped her coffee into the sink. She wished she knew what to say to get back to the easy repartee they'd been enjoying. She didn't like the way Logan could so easily shift from being open to instantly shutting herself off completely from any amiable interaction.

"I'm not judging you."

"It wouldn't matter if you were."

"Would you take me to one of those bars sometime?" Brooke desperately wanted to stay and get to know Logan better, but she knew before Logan responded their evening was over.

"I'll think about it," Logan said before walking out of the kitchen. "But I think you should go now. I have a funeral to direct first thing in the morning."

Brooke left her almost full cup of coffee on the kitchen table and followed Logan to the front door in silence. She wanted to say something—*anything*—to fix things. Instead, she left without a word, and listened to the door click shut behind her.

CHAPTER SIX

Logan sat near the back of the room the next day while Jack delivered his eulogy. He'd let her read through it the night before, and she had to admit it was good. Their father would have been proud of the words Jack had written about him. Logan found herself wishing he was there to hear it. But then again, if he were there, Jack never would have written those words in the first place. The sadness of it all weighed heavy on her heart. Too many people took for granted their loved ones would be around forever. Too many people trusted you could wait until tomorrow to tell them the things you should have told them today. But in reality, nobody was ever guaranteed there would be a tomorrow.

Now *she* was one of those people. She'd never get the opportunity to tell him how much he meant to her. She'd told him she loved him almost every day, but had it been enough? Logan always thought it was, but sitting there at his funeral she knew it hadn't been anywhere near enough.

"How are you holding up?"

Logan looked up to see Ray standing in the aisle next to her seat watching her with concern in his eyes. She tried to smile but quickly gave up and moved over so he could sit next to her. Jack was in the midst of retelling the story about how when he was ten, their father took him fishing for the first time. What a disaster that had been, but the story always made her smile. Jack had hooked a huge walleye, and not really thinking the fish would fight, Jack fell off the boat in his attempts to reel it in. Their father was forced to jump in to save him because Jack had always been an unathletic, scrawny little kid who'd never bothered to learn how to swim. He hadn't *filled out,* as their mother used to say, until he was fourteen. "I'll be okay," she said. She kept her voice down so she wouldn't disturb anyone listening to Jack speak. "Thanks for asking though."

"Missy wanted to know if you and Jack would like to come over for Thanksgiving dinner."

Logan shook her head and glanced over at the Colliers. "Peggy already invited us to their house, but thank you anyway. You know Jack though. He might want to eat a second dinner."

Ray laughed and then coughed in a feeble attempt to cover it. He put an arm around Logan's shoulder and squeezed briefly.

"You're both welcome anytime."

Logan watched him walk back to where Missy and Billy were sitting. Billy gave her an encouraging smile and she tilted her head in acknowledgement. She sat there for a few more minutes before getting up and leaving the room, forcing herself to walk at a normal pace until she was clear of any curious eyes, then she took the steps to her apartment above the funeral parlor two at a time.

She went straight to the kitchen and grabbed the bottle of tequila from the cupboard. After pouring a shot, she stood there with her hands on the edge of the counter for a moment simply staring at the drink. She was stronger than this. Drinking to dull the pain was never a good idea, and the rational part of her brain knew it. But it was so tempting.

Her grandfather on her mother's side had found death in a bottle before Logan was born. Her mother used to tell her and Jack about him all the time, and Logan could never get over the profound sadness she saw in her mother's eyes every time she'd talk about her father. Logan really didn't know if alcoholism was hereditary, but then again, she'd never wanted to find out. She picked the shot glass up and held it at eye level for just a second before dumping it into the sink. She then proceeded to pour the remaining contents of the bottle down the drain as well.

It wasn't like she had decided never to drink again, but having alcohol in the house when the pain was this intense could be a bad thing. She promised from there on out she'd keep nothing in the house but beer, and only a six-pack at most. They might not be with her, but she wouldn't want to let her parents down.

❖

"You disappeared before my eulogy was finished," Jack said when he came up to the apartment a while later. "Is everything all right?"

Logan was sitting on the leather couch in her living room watching an episode of *Dexter* she'd already seen. She and her father watched every episode together, and it had been the last one he had seen. She nodded without looking away from the screen.

"What are you drinking?" Jack asked. He walked over and picked the glass up to sniff the contents. He wrinkled his nose at it. "Water?"

"What's wrong with water?"

"Nothing. I just thought maybe you'd want something a little stronger. I know I sure as hell do. What've you got?"

"Water, soda, and coffee. If you want coffee you'll have to make it yourself. If you want anything stronger, you'll have to go somewhere else." Logan finally shut the television off and turned to watch him in the kitchen. He was looking through the cupboards, apparently not believing she didn't have anything alcoholic on hand.

"There's an empty tequila bottle here in the sink," he called as he continued his search. "Did you drink it all or what?"

"Or what," she said, getting up to join him. She picked the bottle up and deposited it in the recycling bin. Jack stopped what he was doing and turned to face her. She shrugged. "There was half a bottle there. I saw myself sitting here and drinking it all, so rather than risk becoming a lush, I dumped it."

"Is there something you want to talk about?" he asked, his voice full of brotherly concern.

"No, I just envisioned myself drinking too much. Rather than risk developing an addiction to how well it obliterates the pain, I decided to get rid of it. End of story."

He watched her for a few moments to see if she was being honest with him. He opened the fridge and grabbed himself a soda before they went back out to the living room.

"It was a beautiful eulogy, Jack," she said quietly.

"Thanks. I thought so too." Jack put his feet up on the coffee table and stared at the ceiling. "Brooke was looking for you after the service. I take it she doesn't know about the apartment."

"Of course she doesn't. I met her two days ago, Jack."

"You like her though, right? I mean, I thought you'd made picking up women an art form."

"What the fuck is that supposed to mean?"

"You don't want a girlfriend, I get it. I just assumed since you don't want anything long-term, then you probably went for the one-nighters. You can be pissed at me if you want, but am I right?"

"Fuck you." Logan refused to look at him, which apparently was the only confirmation he needed. He laughed. Logan tried hard not to throw something at him.

"I was the same way, Logan. Believe me, I know where you're at. So my question is this—if you're attracted to her, and I'm quite certain you are, why haven't you made a move on her?"

"God, you're a pig." She was having a difficult time admitting to herself Brooke was different. The way she *saw* Brooke was different. Brooke had been hurt deeply by her last girlfriend, and therefore she deserved better than a one-night stand. Logan wasn't the one to offer it to her, and the realization stung, because part of her actually wanted to offer it. Which was crazy, right? *I met her two freaking days ago!*

"All right, fine, I'll leave you alone about it—for now." Jack laughed again and Logan closed her eyes. "Oh, wait, I get it now. You don't bring women here, do you?"

"Would you?" Logan asked before realizing she was feeding into his onslaught. She decided to just go with it. "I mean seriously, how hot is this? I live above a funeral home, for fuck's sake. How many women do you think would bail before we ever made it through the front doors?"

"But the ones who did make it would probably be really hot, don't you think?"

"Or else they'd have some sick fantasies I have no desire to know about." Logan couldn't help but laugh along with him. She loved that he could always make her laugh no matter what was going on in her life.

"So you've really not brought anyone here before?"

"No, I haven't."

"I'm surprised, if you want to know the truth."

"Why?"

"Do you get many women who want to keep seeing you even though you tell them upfront it'll only be a one-time thing?" Jack wasn't laughing anymore, and he turned a little too serious for Logan's liking.

"Yeah," she answered, sobering herself. She'd rather be laughing again. "You too?"

"Yup. I'm a stud. What can I say?"

"No, you're a pig. I thought we already established that."

"You know," he said, blatantly ignoring her insult as he looked around the room. "Bringing them here might be a sure way to guarantee the woman would never call you again."

"You might be right." Logan thought about Brooke. Would she be interested in someone who lived above a funeral home? And really, what did it matter anyway? It wasn't like Logan was looking for someone.

CHAPTER SEVEN

I swear to God, Jack, if one more person brings us a pot of chicken soup I might just take them out back and hang them from the old oak tree," Logan said with blatant exasperation when she set the latest offering down on the granite countertop next to the refrigerator. She never understood people's need to bring food to the grieving family. When her mother died, she and her father hadn't had to cook anything for nearly six months.

"Hey, sis," Jack said, his voice almost a whisper as he cocked his head toward the doorway leading in from the dining room.

Logan whirled around quickly and saw Brooke standing there, a rather large pot in her hands. She looked a little uncomfortable and Logan wondered, eyes darting back and forth between the pot and Brooke, whether Brooke had heard what she said, because Logan knew *exactly* what was in the aforementioned pot.

"Do I get to pick out the rope you're planning to hang me with?" Brooke asked, a smile playing at the corners of her mouth. Logan felt her face flush.

"Colliers are exempt from her threats because Peggy makes *the* best chicken noodle soup in the world," Jack said, saving Logan from what she was sure would have been an embarrassing situation. She watched, unable to move as he went and took the pot from Brooke. "I swear when I went away to college I had withdrawals from this heavenly concoction. I can promise you this soup will not be wasted."

"I'll be sure and let her know," Brooke said with a quick squeeze to his forearm. She refocused her attention to Logan, which caused Logan's face to burn more, if that was even possible.

Their spat after her father's viewing two nights earlier still weighed heavily on Logan's mind. She wanted to talk to Brooke, but she didn't have a clue how to act around her. She'd never tell Jack, but having something else to focus on during the funeral had made everything a little easier for Logan to deal with.

Logan had no clue why she felt so flustered around Brooke, and she'd never had the problem before—ever. She was always sure of herself around women, but Brooke was different. Maybe it was because she hadn't met her in a bar, and therefore her entire world was turned upside down. In a bar, Logan knew the dance, and exactly what was expected. This was a foreign concept to her though. She hadn't been attracted to a woman outside of the bar scene since she'd been in college. And this one wasn't just outside a bar, either. She was on Logan's territory, dropped right into the center of her world.

She finally opened her mouth to say something—precisely what it might be, she wasn't sure—just as Brooke turned and headed back toward the front door. Jack gave her a look of disbelief and mouthed *go* as he pointed to the living room. Logan went, but only because her brother would never let her live it down. It certainly wasn't because she didn't want Brooke to leave. *Yeah, right.*

"Brooke, wait," she said right before she reached for the doorknob. Brooke turned to face her. Logan cleared her throat and looked down at her feet. "I'm sorry."

"For what?"

She should've known Brooke wouldn't make things easy for her. She scratched the back of her neck, a nervous habit she'd started when she was a kid. Logan's eyes landed on everything in sight other than Brooke.

"I was an ass the other night, and I apologize," she said, finally daring to meet Brooke's gaze. "There was no reason for me to react the way I did. I know I shouldn't have avoided you yesterday and today, so I apologize for that also."

"You were an ass the first time I met you too," Brooke said, but she smiled as she said it, clearly as a way to soften her words. "I don't really need an apology, Logan. I'm hoping it's simply a product of your current situation. However, if you continue to be an ass every time we see each other, then I'll probably require some form of compensation."

"What kind of compensation did you have in mind?" Logan winced as she said the words, her mouth obviously working faster than her brain. Flirting definitely seemed out of place, and she made a mental note to not do it again. At Brooke's look of utter amusement, she nodded and shrugged. "Yeah, I'm pretty much always an ass, so you might as well think about what compensation would be required when I run out of apologies."

"I'll keep it in mind." Brooke opened the door but hesitated and turned back to her. "If you ever need to talk about anything, you know where to find me."

"Brooke, wait," Logan said before she had the chance to think about what she was doing. "Will you have dinner with me?"

"Excuse me?"

"Forget it." Logan turned to go back to the kitchen. "Never mind."

"So then you don't want me to have dinner with you?"

"Of course she does," Jack said. Logan looked up and saw the smirk on his face.

"I do," Logan said, turning back to her. "I would very much like for you to have dinner with me. If *you* would like to."

"When?"

"Tomorrow night?"

"Are you asking me, or are you telling me?"

Logan felt her cheeks burning. How the hell did people do this on a daily basis? It was so much easier to walk into a bar and make eye contact with someone. You knew what they wanted, and the dance was already choreographed. This, on the other hand, was nothing short of torture.

"Will you have dinner with me tomorrow night?" Logan asked after a moment.

"I would love to," Brooke said with a smile before walking out the door.

Logan stood staring at the door for a moment before she heard Jack laughing behind her. She gave him her best *shut the fuck up if you know what's good for you* look before pushing past him and going upstairs. She tried not to let his laughter bother her, but he sounded way too happy. She slammed the door to her childhood room before falling face-first on the bed.

❖

"Are you sure you want to go with me to the doctor tomorrow?" Jack asked as they sat down to a dinner of Peggy's homemade chicken noodle soup and Missy Best's freshly sliced, made from scratch French bread later the same evening. "You don't have to, you know. I'm pretty sure I can find my way to Pittsburgh."

"Of course I want to go with you." Logan took her first spoonful of soup and closed her eyes. It really was the best soup she ever tasted. She looked at him with concern. "Unless you don't want me to tag along,"

"It's not like I don't want you there, I just know how hectic things can be for you sometimes, and I wouldn't want you to feel bad for leaving all the work for Billy."

"Billy can handle it, and there's not much going on at the moment anyway." Logan set her spoon down and leaned forward, her elbows on the table. "I want to be there with you when you get the news you'll have to be ready for training camp next July."

"We can always hope, right?" He concentrated on his soup then and wouldn't meet Logan's stare. "I don't want to inconvenience you, Logan."

"You are anything but an inconvenience, little bro." Logan caught his gaze when he finally looked up at her. "I want you to know you're welcome here as long as you want, or need, to stay. I wouldn't admit this to just anyone you know, but I kind of like having you around."

"You just like having someone you can boss around," Jack said with a grin. "Admit it."

"You know me too well."

"You know, you could get the same thing with a girlfriend."

"Really? We're back to that again?"

"When's the last time you had one? And I mean a *real* girlfriend. Not some woman you picked up and spent a few hours with."

"I was twenty-one. It ended badly, and I've never met anyone else I wanted to get so completely involved with again. And not that I want her to be my girlfriend, but I did ask Brooke out, right?" Logan finished her soup and placed her hands palm down on the table. It was the first time she'd mentioned her relationship with Julie in college to anyone other than Brooke. "Your turn. When's the last time *you* had a girlfriend?"

"I have one now," Jack said. "I'm head over heels with this one, Logan. I really can't wait for you to meet her."

"Why didn't you bring her here?" Logan felt the lump forming in her throat but tried to swallow it. Why did everyone want to be paired up with someone? Why couldn't more people be happy simply by themselves?

"I didn't think it was appropriate. I'd never mentioned her to you or Dad, and it somehow felt wrong to show up here with her by my side."

"She told you to say that, didn't she? Because what just came out of your mouth doesn't sound like something you'd come up with on your own. It's a little too cerebral for your feeble mind." Logan laughed when he gave her a mock look of disbelief. "I think I like her already."

"Good, because I invited her here for Thanksgiving."

"What's her name?"

"Cynthia."

"You'd better tell me more about her. I don't want to look like a fool when I meet her and know nothing more about her than her name. Where'd you meet? How old is she? What does she do for a living?"

Jack just looked at her as though she had two heads. Getting information out of him had always been a monumental task. After a few seconds, he shrugged.

"I think I'd rather you get to know her on your own. That way you have no preconceived notions about her."

"Too late for that, bro. She must be an idiot to get involved with you."

They finished their meal and did the dishes with very little conversation. Logan was happy to learn Jack had found someone he wanted to spend his life with. She felt selfish for wanting to keep her brother to herself. Maybe trying to avoid relationships with people wasn't the smartest way to live her life, but after twelve years of it, it was the only way she knew how.

"Why are you here anyway?" Jack asked when they'd finished with the dishes and settled on the couch for a mindless evening of reality television. She looked at him questioningly. "You have the apartment above the funeral home, so why are you staying here with me? Dad had it built to give you your own space. Don't get me wrong. I love spending time with you. But I don't need a babysitter, Logan."

"I feel closer to him here," she whispered. "I'll go back to the apartment, but for now I feel better being here. And it's not to babysit you, even though you probably do need someone watching after you."

He looked as though he completely understood her reasoning. That was what she loved the most about their relationship. They didn't have to talk a lot in order to understand how the other one was feeling.

"After my second concussion three years ago, I decided I'd better start looking into alternative career choices, just in case. Two concussions in one season was a bit of a wake-up call, you know? I got my degree in mortuary science this past summer. I never got to tell Dad I was doing it. I wanted to surprise you both."

Logan didn't know what to say. She was surprised, but at the same time, it made sense. Her brother, for all his joking around, was a smart guy. She nodded as encouragement for him to go on. He took a deep breath.

"I need to find someone to serve my apprenticeship with."

"You mean in case the news you get tomorrow is bad. You *are* going to keep playing if they say you can, right?"

"Of course."

"Billy's only into his sixth month as an apprentice. I can't see taking on another one." Logan saw the disappointment in Jack's expression but he simply shrugged as if it wasn't a big deal. "If you want to wait six months I'd be more than happy to take you on. I'm pretty sure Ernie doesn't have an apprentice at the moment though. I could give him a call for you if you want."

"Sure, that would be great."

Logan knew he'd rather work with her, but Ernie was a good guy. Their father had known him since they'd gone to school together.

Ernie's funeral home was about fifteen miles away in Riverside, which was farther southeast from Oakville, which also meant it was farther from any of the larger cities too. She couldn't help but wonder how well Jack would adjust to living the small town life again.

"We'll wait and see what the doctor says tomorrow before I call him, all right?"

"Sounds good."

They watched television in relative silence for the rest of the evening, and Logan couldn't help but think about how nice it was to have him home again. She hated all the circumstances that had conspired to make his homecoming happen, but she wouldn't lie by saying she wasn't happy to have him back home. She hadn't realized just how alone she really was.

CHAPTER EIGHT

Logan was a little apprehensive when Jack told her he'd called his girlfriend, Cynthia, and invited her to meet them for lunch in Pittsburgh after his appointment with the specialist. The doctor had run some tests and promised to call in a couple of days with the results. Patience had never been Jack's strong suit, and Logan knew sitting around waiting for the phone to ring was going to drive him crazy.

When they walked into the restaurant, Cynthia was already seated, and she waved in their direction. Jack waved back, and when he looked at Logan he had the sappiest grin on his face. She couldn't help but laugh at him as she clapped him on the back and motioned for him to lead the way.

Logan stood back and watched in uncomfortable silence as they hugged, and Jack kissed Cynthia on the cheek. Once they were all seated and they'd ordered drinks, Logan took the time to really look at the woman her brother seemed to be so in love with.

Cynthia was about the same age as Jack, and her long blond hair was pulled back in a ponytail. She wore minimal makeup, which impressed Logan, because so many of the women who made it their life's ambition to hook up with a sports star wore way too much of the crap. Cynthia seemed understated and elegant, and Logan had to admit they made a rather striking couple. She was sure they'd make beautiful babies together. Beautiful blond-haired, blue-eyed babies, which was what their mother always said she wanted for grandchildren.

"I was so sorry to hear about your father," Cynthia said to Logan when the waiter brought their drinks. "Jack's told me a lot about both of you."

"Funny, he never said a word to me about you." Logan kicked Jack's shin under the table. To his credit, he showed no reaction. "It's very nice to meet you though."

"You're a funeral director, right?" she asked. When Logan nodded, she continued. "What an admirable profession. Not everyone is cut out to do that sort of thing."

"And what is it you do for a living?" Logan asked. She wanted to kick Jack again. She hated making small talk, and he was just sitting there smiling like a pig in shit.

"I'm an attorney."

Logan wanted to reciprocate the *admirable* remark, but she couldn't bring herself to do it. For some reason *admirable* and *attorney* just didn't go well together in her mind.

"How did the two of you meet?" Logan wondered if Jack had gotten into the sort of trouble you needed an attorney to get you out of.

"We met at a Cleveland Indians game a few months ago." Cynthia reached for his hand, which was on the table. "He spilled beer on me."

"Still Mr. Smooth with the ladies, aren't you, Undertaker?"

"I had no clue someone was standing right behind me," he said in his defense. He finally managed to look away from Cynthia and focused on Logan. "Beer etiquette states if you have a beer in your hand, the closest person should stand at least two feet from you."

"You're so full of it." She turned her attention back to Cynthia, who she had to admit was much nicer to look at than her brother. "So, he spilled his beer all over you. Let me guess—he made sure to give you his number so you could call him with the cost of the dry cleaning, am I right?"

"How did you know?"

"He's my brother, and it's exactly the same thing I would have done." Logan grinned and took a sip of her beer before looking over the lunch menu. Jack was so obviously happy with Cynthia it almost made Logan nauseous. But she knew before their lunch was even over she was definitely going to like this woman.

❖

"So I'm confused about something," Brooke said when they were at dinner later the same evening. "Did you live with your father? I asked you before why I'd never seen you when I'd come to visit my grandparents."

Logan took a sip of her water and tried very hard to ignore the way Brooke's dress clung to her. And the amount of cleavage she had on display. Her blue eyes were a shade lighter than the dress, and Logan was having a difficult time keeping her eyes above Brooke's neckline.

"No, I don't really live at the house. I've been living in an apartment over the funeral home for the past ten years." Maybe it was time to test out Jack's theory about a woman not wanting to see her again after finding out where she lived. "We probably never saw each other because after my mother died my father didn't want to be around the house on holidays, so we usually went to Florida for Christmas. On Thanksgiving, we went to a movie and ate dinner at a restaurant. He was still holding out hope the apartment would be for Jack when he started building it, but then Jack displayed his uncanny ability to chase down and annihilate quarterbacks. I moved in there when I started working with him."

"If Jack was supposed to take over the family business, how did you get roped into it?" Brooke didn't miss a beat, but Logan thought she saw an uncontrolled shudder run through her.

"I didn't get roped into it. When it became apparent Jack was headed to Penn State on a full ride scholarship, I knew he wouldn't be thinking about the mortuary business for his time there, so it would be at least six years before he was ready to move back to Oakville and work with our father—if he was ever ready at all. I took it upon myself to change course and become a funeral director. So, when our mother died, I moved back here to help him out and I've been here ever since."

"How long ago was that?"

"Fifteen years."

"What was your major before the switch?"

Logan watched in fascination as Brooke took a sip of her water and a tiny droplet ran out the corner of her mouth. It was all she could do to keep from brushing it away with her thumb, but Brooke wiped it with her napkin before she could even think to move her hand.

"Medicine. I wanted to be a doctor. I wanted to heal people instead of bury them." Logan moved back when the waiter brought them the bottle of wine she'd ordered. He poured a glass and waited while she took in the aroma and tasted it. She nodded her approval and he poured their first two glasses.

"Are you a wine connoisseur?" Brooke looked impressed, but the snort Logan replied with left her appearing uncomfortable.

"Sorry," Logan said with a sheepish grin. "Not a connoisseur, no. But my father always told me to at least act as though I knew what I was doing in any given situation."

"Sage advice. Your father was a good man."

"Yes, he was, thank you."

The following silence began to grow uncomfortable and Logan didn't know what to say or do. She sent a silent thank-you to whatever higher power there might be for the waiter bringing their food right before she seriously considered making a run for it.

"Tell me about your father," Logan said when they were left alone to enjoy their meals. She knew it was probably a touchy subject because he'd kept her from seeing his parents for so long, but she wanted to get to know Brooke. What better way than to ask about family?

"He's had his share of troubles," Brooke said.

Brooke met Logan's gaze and Logan saw the sadness there.

"He never talked about his parents unless I asked something specific about them, so I never had any idea what had happened between them. He and my mother are both alcoholics, but in spite of the drinking they were always there for me when I needed them. I guess you might call them functioning alcoholics. They both work full-time jobs, and as far as I know they never drink before five o'clock. I didn't dare bring home any friends from school though because sometimes things got a little ugly once they got home and started drinking. They argue incessantly when there's alcohol involved."

"How did you connect with Henry and Peggy?"

"My aunt Marlene found me. It was my first year of college at Temple in Philadelphia, and she worked in the admissions department. When she saw my name on the roster for that year, she got in touch with me. According to her, my father contacted his parents to tell them they had a granddaughter named Brooke, but refused to tell them where we were, and he never got in touch with them again."

"Did they welcome you with open arms when you met them the first time?"

"It was a little awkward at first for all of us, I think. I was glad Marlene was there as a buffer for our initial meeting, but things quickly evolved, and before I knew what was happening, it was almost as though I'd known them forever." Brooke smiled and started in on her food. Logan decided to do the same before her food got cold. Suddenly, the invitation to dinner seemed like a far better idea than she had anticipated.

❖

"I'm surprised you asked me out, Logan," Brooke said when they arrived back at the house. It was a bit chilly out, being only three days before Thanksgiving, but Brooke didn't mind sitting on the front porch for a while. She wasn't sure she wanted their evening to end quite yet. She was enjoying Logan's company, and it was pleasantly unexpected. Her self-imposed celibacy in the wake of Hurricane Wendy was getting old. Why not go out for dinner once in a while with a stunningly gorgeous woman? It didn't really have to mean anything beyond spending a little time together, did it?

"Why are you surprised?"

"Well, you don't strike me as a woman who dates very often. Even if you hadn't told me as much the other night, I would have figured it out on my own simply by how nervous you were when you asked me," Brooke said. "But you should know I'm not really in the market for a relationship after the way my last one ended."

"As you've no doubt gathered, neither am I. You can always use friends though, and there aren't too many lesbians in Oakville," Logan said with a grin, and Brooke could have sworn Logan's cheeks turned a deep shade of red. "In fact, since you moved here, the number of lesbians in town has doubled. But even if there were thousands, I'm sure none would compare to your beauty."

"Thank you." Brooke felt her own face flush at the compliment. She glanced away, not wanting Logan to see her embarrassment. Wendy had never complimented her very often, and she wasn't sure how to react to Logan's flattery.

"Hey, I didn't mean to make you uncomfortable," Logan said.

She placed a hand on Brooke's arm and Brooke felt her pulse spike at the contact. She fought to not pull her arm away. She wanted Logan to touch her. She wanted Logan to do a lot more than that, but sex wasn't something she ever did casually, and certainly never on the first date. But the fact she was even considering sex with Logan was enough to sound the proverbial alarm in her head.

"You're an amazing woman, Brooke, and your ex was a fool to let you get away," Logan said when the silence continued. Brooke could see in her eyes Logan meant the words she was saying, and it caused a hitch in Brooke's breathing.

"How can you possibly know something like that about me?"

"I know you gave up your life in Philadelphia to come here and care for your grandparents. What else would I need to know in order to come to an obvious conclusion?" Logan asked, sounding sincere. "I'm sure you've heard it many times before, but you really are incredibly beautiful. And I should have said it earlier, but when I first saw you tonight my mouth was a little too dry to speak. You look absolutely stunning in this dress."

Brooke did pull her arm away then, fearing what might happen if she prolonged the contact. She didn't trust the way her body was responding to the things Logan was saying. Arousal was something she hadn't experienced in almost a year, and she had to admit, the feeling was rather invigorating. She could definitely get used to it.

"I have not heard it many times before, but thank you," Brooke murmured.

"Then there've been more fools in your past than I thought."

Oh, Logan was laying it on thick. It wasn't like Brooke didn't enjoy being the recipient of her flattering remarks, but she found herself wondering how many other women she'd said the same things to in the past. Or how many more of them were in her future. Was she saying these things to try to get her into bed?

"Thank you for a wonderful evening, Logan." Brooke got up and walked toward her front door, not really trusting herself to resist Logan's charms for much longer. When she turned back to say good night, she was startled to find Logan standing only a few inches away. "I really should be getting inside so I can check on my grandparents."

Logan leaned in and placed a gentle kiss on her cheek. "I had a nice time tonight as well. I hope we can do it again sometime."

"So do I." Brooke mentally slapped herself for sounding so eager. But then again, what would it hurt to spend time with Logan? They were both single, and neither of them was looking for anything permanent. Just because she'd never been into casual sex before didn't mean she couldn't start now, did it?

When Logan nodded and started toward the railing separating her porch from the Colliers', Brooke stopped her with a hand to her forearm. Before she could give herself the opportunity to think about what she was doing, she put her arms around Logan's neck and pulled her against her body. Logan's hands immediately went to Brooke's hips. Logan's beautiful green eyes darkened and when her tongue came out to wet her lips, Brooke stopped thinking.

The kiss was achingly gentle, which wasn't what Brooke had expected at all. Their lips met and she heard herself sigh. She wanted to pull Logan down to the ground and take her right there on the front porch. Instead, the kiss was over before Brooke could think about deepening it.

"I thought we were only going to be friends," Logan said quietly.

"You asked me on a date."

"So I did." Logan wet her lips again, and Brooke thought her knees might give out. "So, do you want a friend or do you want someone to date?"

"Why do I have to decide right this minute? Can't we simply enjoy the evening?"

"If we want to sleep with each other, there's probably no point in even trying to be friends."

"What makes you think I want to sleep with you?" Brooke pulled away as the haze of desire dissipated quicker than it had developed. What the hell had she been thinking? "I swear to God, you've got to be the most arrogant woman I've ever met."

"*You* kissed *me*," Logan said just as Brooke reached for the doorknob. The chuckle she heard before turning to face Logan had the hair standing up on the back of her neck.

"Trust me when I say it won't happen again."

CHAPTER NINE

It was two days later when the doctor finally called with Jack's test results. Jack had been calmer than Logan in waiting for the phone to ring. It was obvious he'd resigned himself to never being able to play again, though Logan refused to go there. But now, while he was on the phone in the living room, she could see by the look on his face there weren't any more Super Bowls in his future.

"Thanks for everything, doc," Jack said and hung up. He sighed and handed the phone to her. "You might as well call Ernie and see if he's interested in helping me with my apprenticeship."

"Damn it, Jack, this wasn't supposed to happen."

"But it did, Logan, and there isn't a thing either one of us can do about it."

"He said you could never play again?"

"No, he said I could, but he strongly advised against it. The decision is mine, Logan. I can continue playing and probably end up with permanent—or possibly fatal—brain damage, or I can move back here and work with you in the family business. Seems like an obvious choice to me. A no-brainer, if you'll excuse the pun."

"You aren't going to be happy here, Jack. You've lived in the city for too long." Logan couldn't believe she was more upset about his career being over than he was. Why wasn't he angry about it?

"It's not like I was in Manhattan, for God's sake. I was in *Cleveland*." He laughed, and gave her a gentle punch to the thigh. "And you know what? I wasn't cut out to live in the city anyway. I've been more relaxed and happy in the past few days being back here with you than I have been anywhere else in the past twelve years. As long as you forget about the reason I made the trip here in the first place."

"You probably have enough money you wouldn't have to work another day in your life. Why would you want to start working in a field you never had any desire to try before?"

"You're right. I probably wouldn't have to work another day in my life. Especially since I signed a new five-year deal last September. I'll be getting five million a year for the next four years, and I won't have to do a damn thing for it. But I do want to work in the funeral business. I know you never wanted to, so this way you can go back to school and become a doctor if you still want to. I'll take over the family business, and you can have the life you planned for. If that's what you want."

She didn't, but his words caused a lump in her throat. She'd given up on that dream when their mother died, and she'd never looked back. She still had her insecurities about being able to keep Swift Funeral Home as successful as her father had, but it was what she was born to do. With Jack there too, she had no doubt they could keep it going for the next generation of Swifts, which opened a whole new can of worms.

"What about Cynthia?" Logan asked. "She might not be too pleased about your move out to the middle of nowhere."

"We already talked about it," Jack said with a goofy grin. "She's working under contract with her law firm in Cleveland, but the contract is up in May, and then she's ready to move out here with me. I've already started looking at property in the area so we can build a house of our own."

"I don't want to be the doomsayer here, but what if things don't work out for you guys? You've only known each other for three months."

"If I didn't know any better, I'd think you didn't want me here."

"You couldn't be further from the truth." Logan paused, trying to find the words to express her apprehension. "I don't want you to regret anything, Jack. You don't have to come back here and help with the business. Personally, I'd love to have you here, but not if you're doing it out of some sort of loyalty to Dad."

"I'm doing it because I want to do it. I'd appreciate it if you'd stop trying to throw all these roadblocks up in front of me. I've thought about this for a while, and it's what I want. Can you just be happy for me?"

Logan nodded, overcome with emotion. Everything in her life had changed so drastically over the past few days, she wasn't quite sure she could deal with any more changes, even good ones.

"And to answer your previous question, this will give us six more months to see how things go. She'll visit here, and I'll visit there. This is it for me, Logan. I can feel it in here," he said with a hand over his heart. "We both want kids, and once she moves here, we'll have time for it. I'm going to ask her to marry me."

"Wow." She was ecstatic for him even though she wasn't entirely sure she liked the idea of becoming an aunt. They'd probably expect her to babysit or something. "I hope she says yes because she seems to really make you happy, but why don't you guys live here? I'll be going back to my apartment eventually, and the house will be vacant."

"No, you'll find someone someday, and she may not want to live above a funeral home. I know I wouldn't want to. Keep the house, and when you get married, you can live here."

"Aside from the fact I have no desire to, it isn't legal in Pennsylvania."

"But it is in New York, and Jamestown isn't so far away," he said with a grin.

She sighed, knowing he would never give up. Her thoughts turned to Brooke, which terrified her, because for a moment she could actually see them walking down the aisle. She shuddered at the thought.

❖

"And get some beer too," Jack called as Logan walked out the front door later that evening.

"Typical man—can't go to the store for himself," she muttered under her breath. The next day was Thanksgiving, and Logan couldn't have been happier the Colliers had invited her, Jack, and Cynthia over for dinner and football. She didn't have a clue whether Cynthia cooked or not, but there was no way in hell *she* was going to attempt a turkey dinner. Maybe a TV dinner, but a whole turkey? She shook her head. "I don't know how people do it."

"Talking to yourself, Logan?" Brooke asked.

Logan jumped what felt like a foot in the air and whipped her head up to glare at Brooke, who was standing by the street next to her car. They'd managed to avoid each other since their dinner date two days before, and Logan had been doing her best to not give in to the pull she felt. At least three times she'd had to talk herself out of going to ring the Colliers' doorbell. Not out loud, of course, because wouldn't Jack have a field day with her then?

"I'm the only one intelligent enough to carry on a conversation with, so why not?" Her heart swelled when she heard Brooke laugh. It was a wonderful, throaty sound, and it made Logan feel lighter than she had in days. She wanted to listen to it forever. *No, I don't. Where the hell did that come from?* "Are you going somewhere?"

"Gram forgot the spices for the pumpkin pie. She's sending me out on my own to try to find some. Forget the fact I've never been out driving by myself here." Brooke turned away and started to unlock her car door when Logan stopped her.

"I'm going to Riverside to pick up some groceries," she said. "Want to carpool?"

Logan waited while Brooke appeared to contemplate the offer. It didn't escape Logan's notice she looked a little apprehensive to get in the car alone with her.

"I won't bite."

"Promise?"

Was Brooke actually flirting with her? Logan walked down the walkway from the house to her car.

"Not unless you ask me to." She tried to hide her grin at the way Brooke's cheeks turned red. She got in her car and waited to see if Brooke would get in too. She wasn't about to beg her to come along. When Brooke finally joined her and was buckled in, Logan turned to her. "Do you have a curfew?"

"What?" Her surprise was evident. "Where exactly is Riverside?"

"Canada."

Brooke reached for the door handle, but Logan's hand shot out to grip her forearm.

"But the Riverside we're going to is about fifteen miles from here." Logan loosened her grip when Brooke relaxed, but she didn't immediately break their contact. She looked down at where she held Brooke and could have sworn she felt a jolt of electricity. She forced herself to let go and started the car.

"Can I ask a question without you getting angry with me?" Brooke asked when they were a few minutes down the road.

Logan's chest tightened. She kept her eyes focused on the road and simply nodded.

"Why are you so against having a relationship?"

The reasons flooded her mind, but she didn't give voice to any of them. They all made sense to her, but she knew if she tried to articulate them to anyone else she'd no doubt come across sounding like a scared little girl. That was definitely *not* the image she wanted to portray to Brooke Collier.

"Are you going to answer me?" Brooke asked after a few minutes of uncomfortable silence.

"I said you could ask the question. I never said I'd answer it."

"Wow, you must have been hurt pretty badly."

"I've had one girlfriend my entire life," Logan said. She did her best, but it was nearly impossible to keep the defensive tone from her voice. "I told you we broke up. It was because her father died, and she couldn't deal with it. She couldn't allow me close enough so I could help her get through it. Death ripped us apart as completely as it would have if she had been the one who died. Death annihilates everything in its path. It destroys the people left behind. I've seen it time and time again in my profession, and I've experienced it firsthand."

"So you're afraid if you fall in love you'll lose her to death." Brooke shook her head and looked out the window.

They didn't speak the rest of the way to the store, and did their shopping in silence. Brooke had been mulling it all over in her mind, and she couldn't come up with any better explanation than Logan was a coward. She wasn't willing to risk putting her heart on the line because of the possibility death could snatch it away from her one day. But didn't she realize some people spent their entire lives together? Brooke's grandparents were approaching their sixtieth anniversary.

"So it's easier if you never fall in love with someone?" she finally asked. Logan glanced at her, the expression on her face indicating she had no idea what Brooke was talking about. Brooke took a deep breath before trying to elaborate. "How can you possibly think living on your own is a better way of life than having someone to share it with?"

"I seem to recall you not wanting to get involved with anyone either. I thought we were on the same page as far as relationships are concerned," Logan said, obviously wanting to be argumentative. "Besides, how is what I feel any different from what you're feeling? You were hurt badly—it almost killed you, you said—and you don't want to risk it again. Aren't you living like it's easier to never fall in love again? At least my way I'm never alone unless I want to be. I could drive to a bar tonight and find a woman to go home with. What do you have? Your own hand? Maybe some toys in your nightstand?"

Brooke wanted to lash out at her. In that moment she was certain she'd never wanted anything quite so badly. But what would be the point? Why couldn't they seem to spend more than a few minutes together without arguing? She wanted a friend in this town, but clearly Logan Swift wasn't going to fit the bill.

❖

"Oh, my God, that woman is infuriating," Brooke said to no one in particular when she entered the house, hanging her coat up roughly. "I swear I could wring her neck."

"I wouldn't recommend strangulation as a solution to any problem, dear," her grandmother said with a chuckle. She took the bag from Brooke and motioned for her to have a seat at the kitchen table. "What's Logan done now?"

"How—"

"I've had the very same reaction toward her many times," her grandmother said. She waved a hand and took her seat across from Brooke. The smile on her face was one of true affection. "She can be more stubborn than a mule, that one, but she's got a heart of gold. You could do worse than to get involved with her."

"What?" Brooke almost choked on the glass of water her grandmother gave her. She'd never told her grandparents she was gay. They'd come from a different time, a time where things like homosexuality were never spoken of. It wasn't as though she didn't think they could handle it, but she was worried they wouldn't be able to understand. Her own parents didn't understand, so how could she expect her grandparents to? "I don't know what you're talking about."

"Don't be coy, dear. We suspected you might be a lesbian the moment we met you, but certain things over the years have only served to convince us we were right."

"You and Grandpa talked about me when I wasn't here? About my sex life?" Brooke felt her cheeks flush, and she wanted desperately to find a rock to hide under. Her almost eighty-year-old grandparents discussing her private life was more than a little disconcerting. "God, I've never been so embarrassed in all my life, Gram."

"Oh, please, there's nothing to be embarrassed about," her grandmother said with a dismissive wave. "Everyone has sex, right? I'm sure you never got the support you needed from your father, and I always hoped you'd tell us on your own, but catching you off guard like this was a hoot."

Brooke knew her mouth was hanging open, and there wasn't a damn thing she could do about it. Her mind was reeling. When her grandmother laughed at her expression, it was all Brooke needed to snap out of it.

"I think this is only the second time you've mentioned my father," she said quietly. "I've asked him numerous times and he refuses to tell me anything. What happened to cause this rift between you?"

"Rift? It's so much more than a rift, Brooke. It's a chasm I'm afraid can't ever be crossed. The bridges have been burned, and there's no going back." Her grandmother chuckled after a moment. "How many clichés can an old woman cram into a couple of sentences? And what happened between your father and us is a story for another time."

Brooke nodded and tried not to let her frustration show. She was well beyond ever trying to get her father to visit and talk to his parents. It was apparent now, even if he had come, they wouldn't have been interested in anything he would have had to say.

"So?" her grandmother asked, the glint in her eye making her look decades younger. "You and Logan? Am I right?"

"No, you're not. That will never happen because apparently neither one of us is ever going to be in a relationship again."

"Wendy really did a number on you, didn't she? I'm glad you never brought her here, because I'd probably wring *her* neck for hurting you so badly."

"How do you know these things about me?"

"Your aunt Marlene told me. I hope to God you're through with her, Brooke. But if you are, why aren't you interested in another relationship with someone?"

"I am through with her. Don't worry." It was so surreal to be sitting there having this discussion with her *grandmother.* "And the reason I'll never get involved with anyone again is I refuse to let anyone have so much power over me."

"What power is that, dear?"

"The power to break my heart into a million pieces."

"Never say never," her grandmother said with a wink. "You think that way with your mind, but your heart has another agenda, mark my words. You'll fall in love again, because it's what people do. Human beings weren't made to be solitary creatures. You'll find the one meant for you sooner or later. I just hope your grandfather and I are still around to see it happen. You never know—maybe it will be Logan Swift. You could certainly do worse."

Brooke stared at her as her grandmother got up and went about the preparations for her pumpkin pie. She buried her head in her hands and felt an immense sadness engulf her. Her grandmother was right. Her heart did ache at the prospect of spending the rest of her life alone. But Logan Swift? She had to stop the scoff threatening to escape. The woman was a walking time bomb. Even if they did end up sleeping together—which was not going to happen—there was no way in hell anything would come of it. Brooke knew she couldn't put up with the attitude for more than an hour.

But if that were true, why did the thought of sleeping with Logan excite her so much?

This is so not good.

CHAPTER TEN

Logan watched Brooke in silence as she and Cynthia helped Peggy set the table for Thanksgiving dinner. They seemed to be getting along well, which on some level pleased Logan. Cynthia made Brooke laugh more than once, and when she did, Brooke always shot a glance toward Logan, who smiled at her until Brooke looked away again. Logan tried to ignore the feeling in the center of her gut that signaled jealousy. Jealousy over what—because Cynthia was making her laugh instead of Logan? That was ridiculous, wasn't it?

"Logan, are you watching this?" Jack asked. He motioned toward the television where one of the annual Thanksgiving football games was being broadcast. He lowered his voice so Henry couldn't hear what he was saying. "Or are you too busy watching Brooke to care about the game?"

"Actually, I'm watching Cynthia," she said without hesitation. The look on his face was worth the lie, and she turned her attention back to the women setting the table because she knew if she kept her focus on him she'd start laughing. "She's beautiful, Jack. I'm starting to think she might be too good for you."

"You stay away from her," he said, his tone menacing. She did laugh then, but he didn't relax at all. "I'm in love with her, Logan. You'd better stay away from her, you understand me?"

"You are so gullible. Like I'd be interested in a straight woman anyway." Logan sighed and glanced at Brooke. "I can't seem to stop thinking about Brooke."

"What's that?" Henry asked without looking away from the game.

"I said I need to find a good book," Logan said with a wink at Jack.

"No, you didn't," Henry said. "I don't know why everybody seems to think I'm deaf. You go right on thinking about Brooke, because I think the two of you would make a wonderful couple."

Logan was shocked, and she could tell by Jack's expression he was too. She didn't know what to say, so decided to focus on the game and pretend she was the one who couldn't hear.

❖

"Wow, Peggy, you really outdid yourself with this meal," Jack said when he leaned back in his chair and patted his belly. "I don't think I could force myself to eat another bite."

"Good," Logan said as she stood and began picking up everyone's dirty plates. "More pie for the rest of us then."

"Well, I guess I might still have enough room for pie." Jack glanced around the table with a grin as everyone laughed.

When they were done with dessert, Brooke started putting the leftovers away and doing the dishes while everyone else retired to the living room to finish watching the game. She'd just filled the sink up with soap and water when she felt someone watching her. She turned to find Logan against the doorjamb, her arms crossed over her chest.

"More pie?" Brooke asked as she dried her hands on the dish towel she'd slung over her shoulder. "It's in the fridge."

"No, thank you." Logan pushed off the wall and went to stand next to her at the sink. She pulled the towel out of Brooke's hands and watched her for a moment. "You wash and I'll dry. Does that sound all right to you?"

"You don't have to—"

"I want to."

They stood there staring at each other until Brooke thought she'd either have to kiss her or explode. She finally forced herself to look away. Neither of them spoke for a few minutes, but then Logan cleared her throat.

"I'm sorry. I seem to be apologizing to you a lot, don't I?"

"Yes, you do." Brooke glanced at her. It apparently wasn't the answer Logan had expected, but to her credit she didn't miss a beat.

"What I said last night in the car was insensitive."

"The comment about my hand?"

"And the toys." Logan reminded her. She stopped drying the plate she had in her hand and turned to Brooke.

"I do have toys," Brooke said and immediately felt her cheeks flush. *Fuck, did I really say that out loud?*

"Really? Maybe we should try them out sometime."

Brooke threw the dishcloth at her and was satisfied with the wet thump it made when it hit her squarely in the chest.

"Do you enjoy pushing my buttons?"

"I'm sorry."

"No, you're not, because if you truly were sorry, then you wouldn't say some of the things you say in the first place. Maybe you should try thinking before you speak. I know it's probably a foreign concept to you, but seriously, give it a try sometime."

"Look, can we start over?" Logan asked. The look in her eyes indicated she was being sincere, but Brooke wasn't entirely sure she could trust her. "Can we maybe pretend the past week never happened?"

"I don't think I can. Every time we spend any time together, you always succeed in pissing me off. I honestly don't think starting over is going to change that, do you?"

"Probably not."

"Then maybe we should just decide to move on and learn from the mistakes we've both made. It can't be that hard, can it?"

Brooke wasn't sure she believed the words herself, so how could she expect Logan to? If Logan wasn't so infuriating, she'd probably be the type Brooke would pursue. Brooke sighed.

"A penny for your thoughts," Logan said before nudging her with her hip.

Brooke sucked in a breath at the unexpected contact. Why the hell did Logan affect her as much as she did? Anyone else who acted this way she'd simply push to the side and go on with her life. For some reason, Logan had managed to get under her skin in an incredibly short amount of time, and it irked her.

"My thoughts aren't worth so much, trust me."

"I don't believe that," Logan said gently. "They're worth much more than a penny to me."

Brooke wanted to believe her, she really did. But how do you believe a woman who's already admitted to you she goes to bars and picks up women she never has to see again? She turned to face Logan, her hands on her hips.

"See? This is what I'm talking about. You say things like that, and then I'm never sure if you really mean them, or if it's simply a part of your arsenal."

"I have an arsenal?"

"Your list of pickup lines for getting into the pants of the women you meet in bars."

"Ah—that arsenal." Logan leaned against the counter. "Brooke, I've never used a line on you. I'm sure you don't believe me, but it's true. I like you too much to use a line on you. And just for the record? You've done your fair share of pissing me off too. I think you enjoy pushing my buttons as much as I enjoy pushing yours."

"So you do enjoy it then."

"Honestly? I'd rather flirt, but then we end up going down the path to being pissed off anyway."

"Then stop flirting."

"I can't help it when there's a beautiful woman to flirt with," Logan said. "You might as well ask me to stop breathing."

Brooke gave up. Trying to talk to Logan was about as successful as banging her head against a brick wall, headache included. She went back to washing the dishes in silence.

CHAPTER ELEVEN

"Where are you going?" Brooke asked when Logan emerged from the house carrying a small overnight bag.

The football games were over, the turkey was eaten, and too much pumpkin pie was consumed by all in attendance at Thanksgiving dinner. Logan, Jack, and Cynthia had returned to their house an hour earlier, and now Logan was leaving for her apartment. Brooke stood from where she was seated on the glider and moved to the railing.

"Cynthia's staying here for the weekend, so I'm going home. I'm sure they don't want me in their way." Logan had a mischievous thought and set her bag down. "Want to come over and see it?"

Logan laughed when Brooke took a step back from her, shaking her head vigorously.

"I don't understand how you can live in a funeral home," Brooke said with a visible shudder.

"I don't live *in* the funeral home. I live in an apartment above it." Logan was glad they were talking. She'd been concerned after washing the dishes with Brooke she might never speak to her again. "I work there without a problem, so what's wrong with living there too?"

"It's creepy."

"It's a little unconventional maybe, but creepy? No," Logan said as she picked up her bag again. "Well, unless you want to count the times I hear footsteps from downstairs in the middle of the night."

"You're joking, right?"

"Not at all. The strange thing is when I go down to investigate, there's never anyone there, but the door to the cooler we keep the bodies in before burial is always ajar." Logan laughed at the look on Brooke's face and decided to stop teasing her before she got really angry. "Relax, I'm just kidding. It's been my home for the past ten years, so I really don't see anything wrong with it."

"You invite women there just to get this reaction from them, don't you?" The flicker of humor in Brooke's eyes was welcome, but for some reason Logan couldn't let her think what she assumed was the truth.

"I've never invited a woman there, for your information."

"Then why me? Why now?"

Logan shrugged and scratched the back of her neck. Why had she extended the invitation? She enjoyed Brooke's company, that's why. Yes, they always seemed to end their time together with one of them mad as hell, but their interactions were nothing short of invigorating. Brooke made her feel things she never thought she could feel, and she liked it. Even though she hated it, she *liked* it.

"You're different from anyone I've ever met before," Logan said quietly. "You don't let me get away with anything. Women usually take the things I say at face value, and they don't argue. All they care about is what I can give them. They want to sleep with me. To finally meet a woman I find attractive—without the pretense of sex—it's refreshing."

"You mean it's a challenge."

"There's that, too." Logan laughed at her candidness. She took a deep breath and headed down the stairs. "You know where the funeral home is. The invitation is there. Anytime you want to drop by is fine."

"I wouldn't want to disturb a tryst, so don't count on me showing up there."

"I meant it when I said I've never invited anyone there. If I'm home, then you can be assured I'll either be there alone, or with someone who's only a friend. You'll never walk in on something intimate."

Brooke said something else as Logan closed her car door, but she didn't hear it. She didn't bother to look at her either, she simply started the car and drove away. It was one of the few times they'd managed to have any kind of conversation that ended on a somewhat positive note. She wanted to keep it that way, so she chose not to hear what Brooke had to say.

She and Jack had come to an understanding. When Cynthia was visiting, Logan would stay at her apartment. When Cynthia wasn't there, Logan would stay at the house with Jack. It was a good combination for her. She got time with her brother and time to herself. So why had she hoped Brooke would take her up on her offer? She tried to focus her mind on something else.

Maybe it was time to hit the bars again. A little mindless fun with someone she never had to see again might be just the thing she needed to get thoughts of Brooke out of her head. Because she hadn't believed what she'd said to Brooke earlier about there being no pretense of sex between them. Logan definitely wanted to be intimate with Brooke, and she was convinced Brooke wanted to sleep with her. The only problem? Brooke didn't seem to know it yet.

"She finds me attractive?" Brooke whispered with a strange sense of contentment as she watched Logan driving away. She shouldn't be feeling content. She should be running away screaming. But there was something about Logan that kept her on her toes. Something that made her realize life could pass her by if she wasn't paying attention. Brooke wrapped her arms around herself and suppressed a shiver that had nothing at all to do with the cold. Maybe she should've taken Logan up on her offer to visit her apartment.

She shook her head and resumed her seat on the glider. She wouldn't want to give Logan the wrong idea, would she? No matter how captivated she was, she couldn't convey the message she was interested. Because when it came right down to it, she wasn't. The last thing she needed was another woman who wasn't going to stick around.

Brooke had never been able to make a relationship last more than three years. Maybe it was her own fault Wendy had looked elsewhere for satisfaction. No, Brooke thought, she hadn't been at fault. Wendy had never told her she wanted children, so how could Brooke be to blame for what happened? If they'd talked about it, then Wendy would have known she wanted children too. Things might have worked out for them. But maybe the fact Brooke never mentioned it either made it her fault after all. No, she refused to go down that road again.

She sighed, trying hard not to think about the devastation she'd felt the night she'd come home to find all of Wendy's things gone. It had come out of the blue. There'd been no indication whatsoever there might be a problem between them. Brooke left for work after they'd shared a shower—a rather steamy one at that. Everything had been fine right up until she'd arrived home from work.

She waited for the tears that always seemed to come when she recalled the emptiness she'd felt, but they didn't come this time. Only time would tell, but Brooke had the feeling she was finally and completely over Wendy Morris.

Now if she could just stop thinking about Logan, everything would be fine.

❖

It wasn't the first Thanksgiving night Logan had ended up in a bar, so she knew it would be packed with people who either hated the family get-togethers, or who'd had enough of the holiday togetherness and needed to blow off some steam.

Logan got herself a drink and made her way to a darkened corner of the room where she could sit on a barstool and observe the crowd in private. She focused her attention on the dance floor. There was something so utterly sensual about two women dancing together. She took a drink of her beer. An image of her on the dance floor with Brooke in her arms flashed through her mind. Maybe she should take Brooke to a bar some night with the pretense of introducing her to the local nightlife.

What was it about Brooke that had her so preoccupied? She'd wanted to come here to forget about her, and instead Brooke was all she could think about. She felt like a sixteen-year-old girl with her first crush. Thinking about a woman all the time was definitely not on her agenda. It just couldn't work if your plan was to spend the rest of your life alone.

Logan was almost relieved when she heard a noise from her right indicating she wasn't alone in the corner. A hand gripped her forearm lightly, and she felt hot breath in her ear as a familiar body pressed up against her side.

"I knew I'd find you here tonight, lover." The words were followed by a tongue caressing the curve of her ear. She knew the throaty voice and she tried to pull away, but Gretchen's firm grip held her in place. "I've missed you, baby."

"I told you I couldn't see you anymore," Logan said. Gretchen moved around so she was standing in front of her, and Logan had nowhere to go. Gretchen pressed herself firmly between Logan's legs.

"We all say things in the heat of the moment we don't mean, Logan." Gretchen thrust against her slowly. "You know we're both here for the same reason, so why not come home with me? Haven't you missed me?"

No, she hadn't, but she knew better than to say it out loud. She concentrated on keeping her breathing even and trying to convey to Gretchen what she was doing had no effect on her. The reality was what she was doing—the incessant undulating between her legs—was turning Logan on. She let her eyes take in the woman before her. Gretchen was beautiful in a pinup girl sort of way, which made the naughty nurse fantasy a reality when she was in her uniform. Her auburn hair hung in waves to just below her shoulders, and her green eyes shone with mischief no matter what she was doing. Would it really be so bad to go home with her? Her mind was screaming *NO! You can't!* but her body was sending an entirely different message. Gretchen smiled knowingly.

"No strings," Gretchen said, moving in so her mouth was next to Logan's ear again. "I get it, baby. No promises of tomorrow, no expectations of anything beyond tonight. I know what you need, so why don't you let me give it to you?"

Logan closed her eyes and swallowed hard, knowing she would probably end up going home with Gretchen, even though the voice in the back of her mind kept telling her it was Brooke she wanted to be with. She closed the door on the voice and stood, causing Gretchen to almost fall backward. Logan caught her and held her up. Gretchen's arms went immediately around her neck, pulling their bodies together.

"You feel so good, baby," she said, rubbing her cheek against Logan's shoulder before kissing her on the lips. It was chaste, which surprised Logan. Gretchen was usually one to move in for the kill.

"I can't." Logan knew her voice didn't sound nearly as convincing as she'd hoped it would. "I really can't see you anymore."

"Then think of it as a good-bye. Just once more for old time's sake. You know I can make you feel good, Logan."

Logan stood there for a few moments, knowing Gretchen had no clue as to the depth of her internal argument. Her body needed release—more than she could possibly hope to accomplish on her own—but her mind warned this would end up being a mistake. In spite of Gretchen's assurances of no expectations, Logan knew going home with her would send the wrong message, because obviously Gretchen hadn't understood her words the last time they were together. She squared her shoulders and pulled away from Gretchen as she made up her mind once and for all.

"I can't. We've had this discussion already, Gretchen, and I won't have it again. You said before, you could be with me, no strings, and where did that get us? Remember how you took a swing at me when I told you we couldn't see each other anymore? I can't do it. It wouldn't be fair to either one of us."

She left Gretchen standing there slack-jawed as she downed her drink and shrugged on her jacket before walking out the door. Erie wasn't a huge city, and running into an old—what was she exactly? Not a lover, not a friend, but maybe a fuck buddy? God, Logan hated the term, but it fit. They often ended up with each other if they happened to be in the same place at the same time. But running into her just drove home the point she needed to stop going to the bars in Erie. It was a much longer drive, but Buffalo or Pittsburgh were better choices. At least she knew she wouldn't run into Gretchen in either of those places.

CHAPTER TWELVE

It was the following Monday when Logan held open the door to the bar—the very bar Logan had sworn not to go to again—for Brooke and watched her ass sway as she walked in ahead of her. After their fiasco of a dinner date a week earlier, Logan was forced to assure Brooke they would only be going to the bar as friends. How Brooke had managed to get under her skin was something Logan didn't want to spend too much time thinking about, but there was no denying she had.

Logan went to the bar to get their drinks while Brooke snagged a table for them. She saw a couple of women she'd gone home with before, and hoped neither of them would come by their table. She was eternally grateful Gretchen wasn't there to completely screw up her evening. For some reason she didn't want Brooke to think she was a player.

"How often do you come here?" Brooke asked when Logan set her drink down and slid into the booth next to her.

"Not often. Remember I told you I don't like to go out in Erie very often."

"Right. Because you might run into someone you don't want to see again."

Logan glanced at her from the corner of her eye and saw the sly grin on Brooke's lips. She was teasing her. Logan was surprised by the warm feeling in the pit of her stomach at the realization. She couldn't stop the smile tugging at the corners of her own mouth.

"Excuse me," said a rather attractive woman who stopped at their table and leaned across it toward Brooke. "Would you like to dance?"

Brooke looked at Logan, who simply shrugged. It wasn't like they were on a date or anything, so why shouldn't she dance? Logan tried to ignore the jealousy that flared up out of the blue. She looked away when Brooke smiled at the woman. Just because they weren't on an actual date, she didn't have to watch another woman coming on to Brooke, did she?

"I'm sorry, but I'm here with someone."

"You're together?" The woman looked at Logan like she was an idiot. "Doesn't look like it to me."

Logan scooted closer to Brooke and draped an arm around her shoulders. She knew she'd done the right thing by playing along when Brooke placed a hand high on Logan's thigh and leaned in to kiss her on the cheek.

"I'm not buying it," the woman said with a laugh. Her attention was now on Logan. "A word of advice—if I were you, I'd be all over her."

"She's not big on PDA," Logan said. "But thanks for the advice."

The woman walked away with a shrug. Before she got to the bar, she turned back and looked again. Logan waved in her direction and Brooke laughed. Another shot of warmth to her gut shocked Logan and she struggled not to give any outward sign.

"Are you uncomfortable?" Brooke asked, her hand still on Logan's leg.

"No," Logan lied. "Are you?"

"I kind of like how you rescued me."

"I highly doubt you need rescuing, Brooke." Logan started to pull her arm away, but Brooke snuggled in closer. It felt good. Too good. Brooke wasn't the type of woman Logan was used to picking up for a night of fun. She deserved better, and Logan wasn't sure she was equipped to give it to her. But damn if she didn't want to try, at least for the moment.

Logan watched the couples on the dance floor and tried not to think too much about the things she wanted to do to Brooke. The things she wanted Brooke to do to her. The latter thought startled her enough to pull away from Brooke.

"What's wrong?"

"Nothing." Logan wanted out of there. She knew Brooke wasn't ready to go. Hell, they'd just arrived, so she resigned herself to the fact she was going to have to hang out for a while. Her eyes darted around the room, and she had the feeling she was a caged animal looking for a way out. Brooke must have noticed she was spooked.

"Come dance with me."

Hell no, was what went through her mind as a slow song began to play, but before she knew what was happening, she was leading Brooke to the dance floor. She stopped in the center and turned to face her.

Brooke moved into her arms like she'd done it a thousand times before. Logan held her close and felt Brooke's arms go around her waist. Brooke leaned back so she could look up at her.

"You need to relax," she said. "If I didn't know any better I'd think you'd never done this before."

"I haven't," Logan said even though she knew Brooke would have no idea what she was referring to. And she wasn't about to try to explain it. Brooke just gave her a strange look and then shrugged before resting her head against Logan's shoulder.

Logan's heart was pounding, and she was sure Brooke had to hear it even though she gave no indication of it. She closed her eyes and concentrated on trying to even out her breathing, but nothing seemed to be working. The feel of Brooke's body pressed against hers was doing crazy things to her head. When Logan finally thought she might pass out, Brooke pulled away and met her eyes.

"Are you okay?"

Logan nodded. She thought her knees were going to give out when Brooke placed a hand on her cheek and slowly began stroking under her eye with her thumb. When her eyes moved down to Logan's mouth, Logan moaned involuntarily. Brooke's hand moved to the back of her neck and applied pressure, but Logan resisted.

"What are you doing?"

"Trying to kiss you," Brooke said, her eyes never leaving Logan's lips. "You know, in case she's still watching us."

Logan felt the unmistakable rush of arousal and gave in to her desire when she watched Brooke's tongue dart out to wet her lips. She pulled Brooke's body against hers again as she leaned down and their lips met. Tentative at first because she wasn't really sure how far Brooke intended to go with the charade, but when Brooke moved her hand across her shoulder and down to her breast, Logan found herself demanding entry to her mouth. Brooke allowed it and didn't resist when Logan's hands moved to her ass and squeezed gently. They both moaned before Logan pulled away.

"This is so not a good idea, Brooke," she said breathlessly.

"Why?"

Brooke stepped away from her and looked around the dance floor. Logan felt the loss of contact immediately and wished she'd just kept her mouth shut. The truth was, Logan wanted this, but she was scared. She never gave any thought to what she did in the seduction of women, but Brooke was different, and she didn't know how to articulate what she was feeling.

"I'm not good enough for you, is that it?"

"What? No, Brooke." Logan reached for her, wanted to feel her body against hers again, but Brooke swatted her hands away and turned to go back to their table. Logan followed and was surprised when Brooke simply grabbed her coat and purse before stalking out of the club. Logan ran to catch up with her. "Brooke, wait."

"I want to go home now," she said as she stood by the car, her arms crossed over her chest and her attention on something across the street from them.

"Brooke—"

"You pick women up in bars, right? Isn't that what you told me? Jesus, I practically threw myself at you, and you aren't interested. Obviously I'm not good enough for you, so just take me the hell home, now."

Logan stood there staring at her. How could she possibly believe that? She ached to hold her again, to kiss her, to show her how truly attracted she was to her, but Logan instinctively knew it wouldn't matter because Brooke had her mind made up. She opened the car door for Brooke to let her in and then ran around to the driver's side.

They drove home in silence, Logan trying to figure out where things had gone so terribly wrong, and Brooke wouldn't even look at her. She was apparently lost in her own thoughts, and it bothered

Logan to know she was the one who had made Brooke feel like she was lacking in some way.

When she pulled up in front of the house and cut the engine, Brooke immediately grabbed the door handle, but Logan stopped her with a hand on her arm. Brooke finally turned to look at her.

"Let go of me."

"It's me, Brooke. You're not the one who isn't good enough. I'm scared to death I'm the one who isn't good enough for you."

Brooke stared at her as though she had two heads. Logan held her breath while she waited for Brooke to respond. When Brooke pulled her arm away, Logan felt like she'd been slugged in the gut.

"I might have believed you if it hadn't taken you forty-five minutes to come up with it."

Logan's chin fell to her chest as Brooke got out and slammed the door behind her. She wanted to go after her, but what would be the point? Logan knew she would have had the same reaction if the situation were reversed. It was probably for the best if Brooke was pissed at her. A bit of distance was no doubt the best thing for them at the moment. Maybe it would give Logan the time she needed to get her emotions back on track.

Chapter Thirteen

B rooke brushed her teeth after her shower, unable to stop thinking about the fiasco with Logan the night before. What if she'd been telling Brooke the truth? Was it possible she might feel as if she weren't good enough? No. No way. It was a line; she was sure of it.

"You need to stop thinking about her," she said to her reflection. "She's nothing but an arrogant womanizer, and you need to stay away from her."

Not feeling any more convinced than she'd been before she started talking to her reflection, she walked out to the kitchen where she saw her grandmother staring out the window.

"Gram? Are you all right?" Brooke poured herself a cup of coffee, but her grandmother gave no indication she'd heard her. Brooke walked to her and gently placed a hand on her shoulder. "Gram?"

"Good morning," she said absently without looking at Brooke.

"What's wrong, Gram?"

"Your grandfather is having a bad day today."

Brooke's heart sped up. He hadn't had anything but good days since she'd arrived to live with them, so she wasn't entirely sure what her grandmother meant. Bad because of the ALS was something she could handle. Bad because of the Alzheimer's was something she'd never had to deal with. She worked in the ER. Once in a while they'd get a patient with Alzheimer's who had wandered off on their own and gotten injured, but usually by the time they made it to the hospital they were themselves again.

"What can I do to help?"

"Nothing, dear. Just leave him alone. When he gets like this he doesn't remember who anyone is. There's really nothing we can do other than try and keep him calm. I'm just thankful this doesn't happen very often."

Keeping him calm shouldn't be too difficult. They'd told her before she moved in how to deal with one of his episodes. Go with the flow and don't contradict anything he says. She took a deep breath to try to settle her nerves as they sat at the table. She'd never had to deal with Alzheimer patients before, and for the first time she felt woefully inadequate to help her grandmother. They ate their meal in silence, and they were almost finished with the dishes when she heard her grandfather making noises in their bedroom.

"Damn it!" he yelled before a loud crash.

Brooke jumped at the noise, but her grandmother took off for the bedroom. Brooke was surprised she could move so fast. Her grandmother was still relatively healthy, but she was small, and it just seemed as if she should move slowly. When Brooke made it to the bedroom, she stood in the doorway and took in the scene. Her grandmother was trying to help him back into his wheelchair, but he was flat on his back on the floor by his side of the bed.

"Why can't I walk? Who the hell are you and what the hell have you done to me? Why don't my legs work?"

Brooke fought back tears and took a deep breath before her professional demeanor took over. She knelt next to her grandmother and placed a hand on her grandfather's arm in an attempt to still him.

"Let us help you back into the chair and we'll explain."

He looked at her, but she got the eerie sense he wasn't really seeing her at all. He finally acquiesced and allowed the two of them to get him back up. Once he was situated in his wheelchair, he grasped Brooke's wrist before she could move too far away.

"Where is your good-for-nothing brother, Marlene?"

Brooke looked at her grandmother, who was no help at all. She was fussing with a blanket she placed over his legs and refused to look at either one of them.

"I don't know, Daddy," she said, playing along. It was better to not upset him by pointing out she wasn't really his daughter.

"Why were you trying to get out of the chair, Henry?" her grandmother asked as she took a step away from them.

The change of subject wasn't subtle, but Brooke let it go. She would find out the story about them and her father sooner or later.

"Who are you?" he asked. "I don't know you. Where is Peggy?"

"I'm here to help you, Henry," her grandmother said with no emotion, causing Brooke to wonder what it took for her to deal with him in his current state. "Now why were you trying to get out of your chair?"

"I'm supposed to go hunting with John Swift, damn it," he said. "I need to get my guns ready before he gets here."

Her grandmother finally looked at Brooke and motioned for her to leave the room. She did, and her grandmother followed her.

"Go next door and get Logan. Tell her what's happening. When he's like this he always thinks she's her father and it calms him down."

Brooke nodded and ran next door. She knocked loudly before ringing the doorbell three times and knocking again. Logan's car was out front, so she had to be there. She started to knock again but was stopped mid-knock when the door flew open.

"Jesus, what's the emergency?" Logan asked in obvious exasperation. Her expression softened immediately when she met Brooke's eyes, but she apparently saw the worry there because she turned serious quickly. "What's wrong?"

Brooke told her everything that happened, and Logan jumped the railing separating the two porches and walked right into the house. Her grandmother met them and took them down the hall.

"Henry, John's here," her grandmother said before stepping aside and allowing Logan to walk into the room. She placed a hand on Brooke's arm to stop her in the doorway where they watched in silence.

"I hear you aren't ready to go yet, Henry," Logan said, her voice a little lower than it normally was. Brooke watched in amazement as her grandfather's face relaxed.

"John, I don't know why these people won't let me have my shotguns," her grandfather said, his voice barely above a whisper. "They know it's hunting season, and you and I always go out every weekend."

Logan turned his chair so he was facing the bed and she sat in front of him. Brooke couldn't imagine why Logan could calm him down and not her grandmother, but she was willing to try anything because she was having a difficult time seeing him this way.

"Henry, the deer will still be there tomorrow, you know," Logan said. Her grandfather nodded, but he looked disappointed. "I've got a funeral to attend to this afternoon, so we'll go first thing in the morning, all right?"

He nodded.

"Marlene," he said, motioning to Brooke to come over to him. "You'll have my guns ready for tomorrow, won't you?"

Brooke glanced at Logan, who nodded once, before replying, "Yes, Daddy. Of course I will."

"Good girl."

"I'll see you bright and early then, Henry," Logan said as she got to her feet. She leaned down so he thought what she was saying was just between the two of them. "You don't give these ladies any grief, you hear me? They love you, and they only want what's best for you."

Her grandfather agreed but didn't look happy about it. The three of them got him into the bed before they returned to the kitchen where her grandmother fixed Logan a cup of coffee.

"Thank you, Logan," Brooke said.

"No problem. I'm just glad I could help."

"Does this happen often?" Brooke asked. When her grandmother wouldn't look at her, she turned her attention back to Logan. She knew her exasperation was evident, but she tried to sound unaffected by the events of the morning. "It hasn't happened since I moved in here."

"Actually, I think it occurred more often before you arrived," Logan said with an agreeing grunt and nod from her grandmother. "The first time it happened, my dad was out of town at a seminar, and Peggy called me at the funeral home to ask for my help. When I got here, Henry thought I was my father, and I was able to talk him through the worst of it. After that, it didn't matter if it was me or my dad because when he's in this state, he thinks we're the same person."

"Peggy!" her grandfather called from down the hallway. Her grandmother placed a hand on each of their shoulders before taking a deep breath and going to see what he wanted.

"I'm not sure how she deals with it," Brooke said quietly.

"It's not easy, I'm sure." Logan covered Brooke's hand with her own on top of the table, and Brooke didn't move away. "But the good news? He's himself again now."

"How do you know?"

"He called for her. When he's having an episode, he doesn't know who she is and he doesn't always remember he's married."

Brooke looked at their hands and closed her eyes as she turned hers to entwine their fingers together. She squeezed Logan's hand before looking at her again.

"Thank you for being here. Thank you for taking care of them. Thank you seems so inadequate but it's all I have. Thank you for caring about them."

"Hey, they're family. It's what families do, right?"

Was it? Brooke knew without a doubt it wasn't what *her* family did. Her father hadn't seen his parents in over forty years. Brooke couldn't imagine him doing anything to help them.

"I'm sorry about last night, Logan."

"Don't be. If I wasn't so inept at being with a woman I find attractive, the evening may have ended differently."

"Logan," he said from behind them.

Brooke and Logan both turned in their seats to face him. Her grandmother had parked his wheelchair in the doorway separating the kitchen and dining room, and she was standing behind him, her hand on his shoulder and his hand covering it.

"Hey, Henry. Good morning." Logan gave him what Brooke could tell was a genuine smile full of affection. It made the lines at the corners of her eyes crinkle, and Brooke had the fleeting thought Logan was the sexiest woman she'd ever met.

"I want to apologize. Peggy filled in the missing pieces, but you know I remember some of the things I say and do. I'm sorry you had to pretend to be your father again."

"I didn't pretend anything, Henry." Logan got to her feet and went to kneel next to his chair. "If you see my father when you look at me, I consider it a compliment."

Brooke's breath caught in her throat. Logan was an incredibly sweet and caring woman, and Brooke thought it was a shame she didn't share that part of herself with anyone other than family and close friends. Brooke felt honored to be seeing it now. She fought the urge to take Logan in her arms and hold her tightly. When Logan turned her head to meet her eyes, Brooke wondered why she was fighting the attraction she was certain both of them felt.

CHAPTER FOURTEEN

Logan sat in her office looking over the numbers for the year. They were doing pretty well for a small town funeral home. Ernie, who ran his business out of Riverside where there was a much higher population of people, could only dream of doing as much business as she was. Jack had started his apprenticeship with Ernie the Thursday after Thanksgiving, and Logan wished she could have taken Jack on as an apprentice, but she just didn't have the time to do it since Billy still had six months left in his.

"Hey, Boss," Billy said after a quick knock on the open door. "Do you have a minute?"

"Sure thing. Come on in and have a seat." Logan sat back and waited for him to get comfortable. It was amazing how much Billy looked like his father. They had the same green eyes and messy brown hair. He had Missy's nose, which was a good thing since Ray's always seemed to her to be way too large for his face. "What's on your mind, Billy?"

"I was just wondering if maybe I could use the apartment upstairs this weekend."

He was looking everywhere in the room but at her, and she leaned forward. It wasn't like Billy to be nervous about anything. Granted, this was a strange request, but they were close enough to be family. He'd never been apprehensive about asking for something before.

"I live up there, Bill."

"I know, but you've been staying at the house so much lately, and I would really appreciate it if you could say yes."

"What do you need it for?"

He hung his head and shook it, apparently not intending to answer her question.

"You want some alone time with a girl, is that it? I know living with your folks probably cramps your style, right? Especially when you're thirty years old. I can't imagine. I'll tell you what—you can use it for the weekend, but only the guest bedroom. And when I come back Monday morning, the sheets better be clean."

He chuckled nervously before looking up and finally meeting her eyes. "It's not a girl."

Logan glanced away to hide the knowing grin. She thought briefly about not saying anything and simply letting him tell her on his own, but she could see how difficult it was for him. Ray and Missy were great people, but they were devout Catholics. They were fine with her being gay and always had been, but who knew how they might react if they found out something like that about their own son?

"It's a guy?" she asked carefully. He didn't answer right away, so she went on. "Billy, you know I don't have a problem with it, right? I wish you'd have told me sooner though. My dad might have been able to help you come out to your parents. How long have you known this guy you want to bring here for the weekend?"

"A couple months. We met at the grocery store one night when my mom asked me to pick up a few things."

"Why can't you go to his place?"

"He lives with his sister."

"Where have you gone with him before?"

"We haven't gone anywhere. We haven't had sex yet."

Logan couldn't hide her surprise. Two months and they hadn't had sex yet? And people thought gays and lesbians were all about the quick hookups. She wasn't sure she really wanted to know the answer to her next question because it probably fell into the category of *too much information*, but her curiosity was too strong.

"You've had sex before though, right? With a guy?"

"No." He squirmed in his seat. He looked like he wanted to make his escape, but he finally closed his eyes and seemed to relax a little bit. "I've never spent the night with a guy before."

"Have you been with a girl, or are you an honest to God virgin?" Logan asked. Billy was the same age as Jack, and they'd played football together in high school. Billy played his college ball in Ohio and was on track to be drafted in the first round before he blew out a knee. After taking a couple of years to rehab his knee, he'd been forced to make a new career choice. He'd gone through the police academy at his father's insistence, but he knew law enforcement wasn't for him. He'd finally settled on mortuary science. Billy and Jack had been best friends growing up. If Jack knew Billy was gay and never said anything to her, she'd kill him.

"I did once, on prom night. God, it was the most awful experience of my life, Logan."

"I can imagine." She'd never even tried to conform to the societal norms. She'd known from a young age she liked girls and not boys, and never had the desire to experiment. "If you guys stay here for the weekend, what are you going to tell your parents?"

"I'm visiting a friend in Buffalo."

"Clean sheets," she said again.

"I promise," he said, his mood visibly lifting. "You'll never even know we were there."

"I'd better not, or you'll never get to use my apartment again."

"Thanks, Logan," he said before running out the door. A second later he was back. "You won't tell my parents, will you?"

"I would never out someone without their permission. Don't worry about it, Billy. Your secret's safe with me." She smiled as he left again, and she could hear his running footsteps fading down the hallway. She looked at her watch. If she hurried, she could be in Buffalo before nine o'clock. It was a Thursday, so the bar crowds would be fairly decent. She grabbed her coat and shrugged it on before heading for the door, where she literally ran right into Brooke.

"Jesus, are you in a hurry or something?" Brooke asked when Logan steadied her with a hand to the small of her back.

"No, not really," she lied. They had managed to avoid each other since the incident with Henry, never sharing anything more than a hello when they'd see each other. "What brings you here to the creepy old funeral home?"

"You invited me, remember? And you assured me it wasn't creepy."

"I seem to recall inviting you to my apartment, not the funeral home, per se." Logan looked at her watch out of habit, and Brooke apparently noticed.

"You are in a hurry." Brooke appeared disappointed.

"It's nothing important, really. Come in and have a seat."

Logan didn't want to analyze why it suddenly wasn't important to get to Buffalo. Because if she took the time to consider it, she might have to admit to herself she liked Brooke a little too much. Not only that, but she was *intensely* attracted to her. The attraction was okay, but the intense part? Not so much. It wasn't acceptable in the tidy little world Logan had created for herself. She focused on Brooke, who was sitting across the desk from her.

"You really bury people for a living?" Brooke asked, her expression one of distaste.

"Yes, I do. But I'm curious as to why you seem to find it so objectionable. You're a nurse, aren't you? I'm sure you've had to deal with a dead body or two in your line of work."

"Yes, but trying to save people's lives is different than preparing them for burial."

"So you're trying to say your profession is more noble than mine," Logan said. She cut Brooke off when she tried to respond. "It isn't the first time I've heard something similar from someone in the medical profession. As a matter of fact, it was those exact feelings that spurred me toward a career in medicine when I graduated from high school, but we both know how far I got there. My father taught me many things in life, and one of them was to handle each body as if it were a member of your own family, because the deceased deserve to be treated with respect. He told me if I couldn't handle that, then I didn't belong in this business. There are reasons funeral homes are usually family run. Not everyone is cut out to be a mortician. We do it because someone *has* to, and there aren't many who *want* to."

"So you don't enjoy your job?"

Logan held Brooke's eyes for a moment as she considered her answer. Brooke didn't appear to be as uncomfortable as she had been when they first sat down together, and for some reason it pleased Logan.

"I didn't think I would like it at first, but I've come to feel differently about it over the years. What I do is necessary. Do I enjoy it? No, I wouldn't go that far, but I do get a deep sense of satisfaction when I can help a family through the first days—the most difficult days—after the loss of a loved one. Grief is a powerful emotion, Brooke, and most people need someone to listen even if they're not aware that's what they need."

"So you're basically a high-priced therapist."

Logan took a deep breath and tried to calm herself. Brooke was trying to get on her nerves, and succeeding. But she'd never give Brooke the satisfaction of knowing it. Her amusement was apparent in the way her eyes flashed, and Logan was determined this interaction wouldn't end in the way that was fast becoming typical for them.

"I guess you could look at it that way. I'm sure it's probably how most people view the profession. But what we do is so much more. We take care of the obituaries, the flower arrangements, the funeral notices. There's so much involved with funeral preparations most people don't even consider. Because of me, and other people in my position, loved ones don't have to do a thing. We even provide clothing for the deceased if it's what people want."

"You're freaking me out a little bit," Brooke said after a moment. Logan's expression must have conveyed her confusion because Brooke waved her hand in the air toward Logan and shook her head. "You've gone all mortician on me. You're using that soothing voice, and you're using words like *deceased*, and *loved ones*. It's kind of creepy. I want to talk to Logan, not Ms. Funeral Director."

Logan smiled. She hadn't even noticed slipping into professional mode, but it was a natural thing to do. They were talking about funerals, and something in her mind flipped a switch. She remembered being a little creeped out about it herself when she was younger and her father did the same thing. She laughed before standing and walking toward the door.

"All right, Ms. Funeral Director has left for the day," she said. "How about I give you the nickel tour of the place?"

"I'm afraid I don't have a nickel," Brooke said.

"Then for you it's free. Just don't tell anyone. I usually charge ten bucks a head for a tour." Logan smiled when she was rewarded with an all out laugh. She vowed to try to elicit the same response more often in the future. She held her arm out and was pleasantly surprised when Brooke threaded hers through it. A rush of heat flooded her system at the contact as she leaned her head closer to Brooke's. "We'll start with the embalming room."

"You'd better be kidding." Brooke yanked her arm away and took a step back toward the desk. Logan laughed and exited the room.

"Billy should be done with Mr. Granger by now, but I guess I should make sure before we barge right in there." Logan glanced over her shoulder. "I think we'll start our tour with the crematorium."

❖

The tour took almost forty-five minutes, and—much to Brooke's relief—did *not* include a stop in the embalming room or the crematorium. She shivered just thinking about it. Simply looking at the selection of caskets and urns was enough to freak her out for one night.

"Why *are* you single, Logan?" Brooke asked, her mouth acting before her brain could fully engage. Logan stopped walking and looked at her with a funny little grin. "I mean, I know the reason you already gave me, but I can't believe you've sworn off relationships. You'd make some woman a wonderful partner."

"Some woman? I'm not interested in *some woman.*"

The look Logan gave her left the impression she was interested in Brooke, and it caused a flash of heat she felt to her core. It was amazing to her how Logan seemed to have the ability to make her feel as though she were the only woman in the world. Brooke wondered if she had the same effect on all the women she picked up.

"The tour of my workplace hasn't answered that question for you?" Logan asked when the silence had gone on a little longer than was comfortable.

"Because of this?" Brooke looked around the chapel room. It was peaceful, but when she thought about where she was, a chill ran through her.

"No, because of this," Logan said as she ran a finger down Brooke's arm from her elbow to her wrist, indicating the goosebumps Brooke hadn't noticed were there. The move caused even more shivers, and Logan gave her a wink. "I'm used to this kind of reaction, but luckily, most women run away as soon as they learn what I do for a living. I don't generally have to push anyone away."

Brooke hugged herself and ran her hands up and down her arms. She knew it had to be her imagination, but she could still feel where Logan had touched her. This was heading into dangerous territory, and Brooke felt helpless to stop it. She was hopelessly attracted to Logan, and the woman was sexy as hell. She oozed charm when she wanted to, and Brooke was worried if she were exposed to much more of it she might simply dissolve into a puddle of lust at Logan's feet.

"I'm sure you tell women what you do for a living in order to chase them away, am I right?" Brooke knew her response would piss Logan off, and she wasn't disappointed. Logan stiffened and turned away from her. She regretted having said the words aloud and reached out to touch Logan's arm. "I'm sorry. I wish we could spend more than an hour with each other and not have it end this way. I really hate the getting to know each other phase of a new friendship. It would be so much easier if we already knew all the things *not* to say to keep the other one from getting upset."

"Is that what this is?" Logan asked when she turned to face Brooke again. "A new friendship?"

"I hope so. I never thought I'd find a lesbian in Oakville, much less one I could be friends with, but I'm glad I have. Even if we just constantly piss one another off."

"Me too, but there's this pesky little thing about me being attracted to you. That doesn't bother you?"

"No, because we've already established neither one of us wants a relationship. And since I don't do casual, there's no chance of anything happening between us."

"What if I told you I'd be willing to risk it with you?" Logan asked, her voice low.

Brooke's breath caught in her throat and she took a step back. Her first reaction was to laugh at the absurdity of the remark, but the look in Logan's eyes told her she was being sincere. Logan was wearing her heart on her sleeve, so to speak, and Brooke had no idea what to do with the enormity of the situation. She shook her head and opened her mouth, but Logan spoke first.

"You didn't think I was serious, did you?" Logan laughed and walked down the hall to her office. "If you want to be my friend, you'll have to get used to my sense of humor."

Brooke was furious. She was sure Logan's response was a defense mechanism, but it didn't exasperate her any less. Part of her wanted to follow Logan and give her a piece of her mind, but the more rational part of her decided leaving without another word was the more sensible thing to do. Logan frustrated her no end, and she really didn't want to think about the reasons *why* it was so easy for Logan to get to her. There was no way in hell she'd ever let Logan know the attraction was mutual, because she knew she'd never hear the end of it.

CHAPTER FIFTEEN

When Logan walked into her apartment Monday morning, the only thing to make it obvious someone had been there over the weekend were the clean dishes in the strainer by the sink. She never washed by hand. If you were meant to wash dishes by hand, there wouldn't be automatic dishwashers, right?

She walked through the apartment and was pleasantly surprised at how clean everything was. Perhaps she should consider hiring Billy as a housekeeper. Even the extra bathroom was spotless, and there were new sheets on the bed in the guest room.

Her relief was short-lived when she entered the master bedroom though. There was someone in her bed. Billy was downstairs—she'd seen him in the embalming room working, his iPod turned up high enough for her to hear it coming from his ear buds. She glanced at the clock on the bedside table and admitted she was about an hour earlier than usual, but she'd thought they would have been long gone by now. She certainly didn't think Billy would leave his boyfriend alone in her apartment.

She cleared her throat and waited in the doorway as the man in her bed stirred but never opened his eyes. She tried again and a grin broke out on his face, though he didn't open his eyes.

"Come back to bed, Billy-boy," he murmured. He stretched, and the sheet covering him slid off. His hand landed on his chest and began to move slowly down his stomach. Just before it reached what Logan was sure was its destination, she decided she'd seen enough.

"Billy's downstairs working," Logan said, her voice calm in spite of the fact she found the situation humorous. She knew she should be pissed off, but she couldn't help it. "This is my apartment. I do have a suggestion for you though. It might be best for both of us if you were to cover yourself."

His eyes flew open and he grasped for the sheet. Just as he got it over himself Billy came bounding up the stairs.

He came in through the door off the hallway and didn't see her standing in the door leading from the bedroom to the kitchen and the rest of the apartment. She watched in amusement as he ran in, gathered his guest's clothes and threw them at the bed.

"Get dressed and get the hell out of here," he said. "Her car's outside so she's got to be on her way in."

"Too late, Bill," she said from behind him. He whirled around so fast he almost lost his balance. "And I've already seen much more of your boyfriend than I ever wanted to. Get him dressed and out of here, then I want to see you in my office."

She turned to go back downstairs and get to work, but a DVD case next to the television caught her eye. She always kept her movies put away and in alphabetical order. When she got closer she saw the unmistakable picture of two naked men in a very compromising position. She ejected the disc and put it back in the case before tossing it onto the bed.

"And don't forget your movie. Gay porn is definitely not my preferred method of entertainment."

It was an hour later before Billy finally entered her office, his expression telling her all she needed to know. He was thoroughly embarrassed. He looked almost as if he were in physical pain waiting for her to blow up at him for leaving someone alone in her apartment. She waited until he was seated in front of her desk before she spoke.

"Relax, Billy, I was early. I should have figured you'd milk every possible second out of the weekend. I just thank God I didn't walk in on you guys…well, you know. But I specifically told you not to use my room. I hate it when someone else sleeps in my bed, and I know that isn't all you did there if the DVD I saw was any indication."

Billy turned a shade of red Logan had never seen before. She was afraid he might actually pass out.

"I'm so sorry," he said, his voice strangled. "I swear it won't happen again."

"You're damn right it won't, because you won't be using my apartment again." She'd intended on teasing him a bit, but he already appeared to be at his breaking point as far as mortification went. She smiled to let him know she wasn't insanely mad at him, but she couldn't resist one final dig. "I've usually at least been introduced to someone before I see them naked."

"His name is Carl, and I promise next time he'll be fully clothed, and I'll introduce you," he said. "We changed your sheets, and the dirty ones are in the washing machine now. I'll dry them and put them away later."

❖

"Hey, sis," Jack said when he walked into her office and had a seat. He picked up the photo she had on her desk and looked at the image of their parents. It had been taken on the Alaskan cruise they'd gone on to celebrate their twentieth wedding anniversary, which was less than a year before her mother had died. "I always loved this picture of them."

"They were so happy, weren't they?" Logan pushed the paperwork she'd been working on aside and stood to grab a soda from the small fridge she kept in the corner. She offered one to Jack, but he declined. "What are you doing here? Shouldn't you be working?"

"Ernie's got a viewing tomorrow morning. He let me go early today so I could help with it." He leaned forward and placed the photo back where he'd found it. "I thought maybe we could go to Erie and grab some dinner if you don't have other plans."

"Sounds great. Let me call Billy in here to let him know I'm leaving." Logan picked up the phone and dialed the number for the embalming room. She looked at Jack as it rang. "Have you seen Billy since you've been back?"

"Other than Dad's funeral where we didn't even say hello to each other? No. I've been meaning to stop by here and shoot the shit with him, but I just haven't gotten around to it."

"Hey, Boss," Billy said. "What's up?"

"Come to my office please. I need to discuss something with you."

"On my way."

He'd explained to her earlier in the day how it hadn't been his idea to use her bed the night before, but she hadn't cared. There was no television in the guest room, and the king-size bed in the master bedroom was much more comfortable than the queen. She assured him she probably would have done the same thing if she'd been in his shoes. She also made it clear to him—again—that he would never be using her apartment for a tryst. When it came right down to it, if she couldn't trust him to follow one condition, how could she trust him with her home? It was only a few minutes before he walked into her office.

"Jack, how the hell are you?" he asked, a big grin on his face when he walked in. Jack stood and hugged his old friend. The contrast in size wasn't nearly what it was between Jack and Billy's father, Ray. "It's good to see you again."

"You too, Bill," Jack said with a grin of his own. "How've you been?"

"Not bad."

"Married yet?"

"No." Billy glanced at Logan, who simply shrugged. "You?"

"Soon, I hope. We'll have to get together when Cynthia's in town so you can meet her."

"All right, enough reminiscing," Logan said as she grabbed her jacket and put it on. "Billy, I'm going out to eat with my brother. You can handle things here, right?"

"Sure."

"Just call me if you need me."

"Logan, can I talk to you for a minute?" Billy asked before she walked out the door.

Logan waved Jack on and then came back into the office, closing the door behind her since she assumed whatever Billy wanted to say was private. She watched him for a moment before he finally took a deep breath and started.

"I think I need to tell my folks I'm gay."

"Okay." Logan nodded, wondering what he wanted from her. "Do you want me to be there when you do?"

"No, I think if you were there it might be a little awkward for them. I'm just not sure how they're going to take it, you know?"

Logan sat in one of the chairs in front of her desk and motioned for Billy to take the other one. "Don't worry about it, Bill. You have friends. If the unthinkable happens and they throw you out—which I don't think will be the case—you can have my old room at the house. We'll work something out, all right?"

"Thank you. And thank you again for the use of the apartment over the weekend."

"So you're serious about this guy?"

"Yeah. He's pretty amazing. I really want my parents to meet him."

"Make sure he's got clothes on for that meeting. I have a feeling your parents won't be as laid back about it as I was," Logan said. "You aren't planning on having him there with you when you tell them, are you?"

"No." He laughed nervously. "I think I'll tell them tonight after I leave here."

"Good luck. And don't be so nervous. They love you, right? They'll handle it better than you think they will, mark my words."

❖

"They kicked me out."

Logan grabbed Billy by the arm and pulled him inside and out of the snow that had begun to fall earlier in the evening. She took his coat and hung it up before ushering him inside and sitting next to Jack on the couch. Billy took the chair facing them.

"What do you mean they kicked you out?" Jack asked, apparently having overheard. "Why would your folks kick you out?"

Logan watched the emotions pass over Billy's features. She figured he was upset about how his parents reacted to his news, and now he was torn as to whether he should come out to the man who had been his best friend through high school. Logan decided to intervene.

"Billy, can I tell him?" Logan waited for an answer, but all she got was a pained nod before he looked away. "Jack, Billy came out to Ray and Missy tonight."

"No shit." Jack sounded surprised but his grin seemed to be out of place. It occurred to Logan he'd probably already known this about his friend. "It's about time, Billy. Jesus, it really took you this long to figure it out?"

"How—" Billy stopped and the confusion on his face almost made Logan laugh out loud, but she knew it wouldn't be a good idea. He shook his head and started again. "No, I knew our freshman year of high school. I knew beyond a shadow of a doubt when I had sex with Lisa Garrett after the prom. How the hell did you know and why the fuck didn't you clue me in?"

"Please." Jack laughed. "I've known since the day we met. Maybe it's because I have a gay sister. I don't know. Why did it take you so long to tell your parents?"

"They're Catholic," Billy said as though it explained everything, and Logan supposed it probably did.

"You can stay here, right, Logan?" Jack asked.

"Absolutely. You can have my room and I'll go back to my apartment for tonight. We'll work something more permanent out tomorrow, all right?"

"Thank you," Billy said, his relief obvious.

The doorbell rang and Logan got up to go answer it. She couldn't believe Ray and Missy would turn their backs on their own son, and her frustration came through in the way she yanked open the door.

"Bad time?" Brooke asked as she took a step away from the door.

Logan cleared her throat and shook her head. The last thing she wanted was to let her foul mood interfere with the possibility of spending time with Brooke. She gently pushed open the screen door and motioned for her to come in.

"Is everything all right next door?"

"Everything is fine." She turned to face Logan as she shut the door. "I wanted to apologize for the other night. I had no right to be so upset with you."

"I think we spend way too much time apologizing to each other, don't you? As far as the other night, you were only so upset because you're attracted to me and you can't admit it," Logan said, loving the way Brooke's jaw clenched, indicating she was getting pissed again. Logan laughed. "Relax. I'm only teasing you."

Brooke stayed silent and followed Logan into the living room. It was frustrating to realize Logan could so easily bait her. She'd never said the words out loud, but she'd made the vow to herself she would *never* get involved in another relationship. But Logan was different from any other woman she'd ever known. She was slowly but surely breaking down all the barriers Brooke had managed to erect in the past nine months, and while it scared the hell out of her, it also gave her a warm feeling deep in the pit of her stomach.

Brooke hesitated when she saw Logan and Jack had a visitor. She glanced at them before opting to take a seat in the chair by the end table on Logan's side of the couch. Before she could sit though, Jack stood and insisted she take his spot on the couch.

"I'll be fine here."

"Nonsense. This chair is the most uncomfortable piece of furniture in the house," Jack said before gently taking her arm and directing her to the space he'd vacated on the sofa next to Logan. "For some reason, Dad liked it."

"Thank you," she murmured without even a glance in Logan's direction. She could feel Logan's eyes on her, and just *knew* Logan had a self-satisfied grin plastered on her face. Brooke smiled at the other man in the room, whom she had never seen before. "Hi, I'm Brooke."

"Sorry," Logan said as she sat up a little straighter. Brooke spared a glance in her direction and was pleased to see she really did seem to be flustered. "Billy Best, this is Brooke Collier. Brooke, Billy works with me at the funeral home."

"You're Henry and Peggy's granddaughter?" Billy asked. When Brooke nodded in response, he smiled. "My dad told me you were living with them now."

"Your dad?" Brooke asked, feeling completely lost in the conversation.

"Billy's dad is Ray Best, Oakville's Chief of Police," Logan explained. "He's actually the only cop in town, but he likes the title anyway."

"I'm afraid I haven't had the pleasure of meeting him yet," Brooke said. "But it's nice to meet you, Billy."

"You too," he said as his gaze shifted back and forth between Brooke and Logan. He looked as if he'd had an epiphany. "Oh...so you two are, you know, an item?"

"No," Brooke and Logan said in unison. They looked at each other and Brooke felt her heart warm at the brief connection.

"Excuse me for a moment," Logan said and disappeared into the kitchen.

Brooke watched her go, and was surprised she actually had to force herself not to follow her. It was almost as though there was a magnetic pull between them, and Brooke didn't understand it in the least. She cleared her throat and tried to relax. She smiled occasionally as Billy and Jack made small talk, but her attention wandered as she waited for Logan to come back. Her heart rate sped up when Logan walked back into the room, four beers in her hands. She passed them around and took her seat again just as the doorbell rang. Logan smiled—a bit nervously, Brooke thought—and got to her feet.

"Billy, I'm sorry, but this is probably your parents."

CHAPTER SIXTEEN

Billy looked like he was contemplating how to make an escape through the back door when Logan placed a hand firmly on his shoulder. She looked at Jack and urged him to answer the door.

"You called them?" he asked, his voice a strangled whisper.

"No, Bill, I swear I didn't. Your mom called me on my cell while I was in the kitchen." Logan squeezed his shoulder and leaned down to look him in the eye. "She was upset about how things went tonight, and she begged me to let them come over and talk to you. They figured you had come here when you left. We can give you guys some privacy if you want or we can stay and be your moral support. Completely up to you, all right?"

"Please stay." He closed his eyes and swallowed audibly just as Jack reentered the room with Ray and Missy Best following.

Logan pulled Missy into a warm hug before kissing her on the cheek and offering her a seat on the couch. Ray gave a quick nod in Logan's direction before sitting next to his wife. Brooke stood and headed toward the door.

"I should go," she said by way of apology.

Logan stopped her with a subtle shake of her head. She made introductions before asking Jack to get a couple of the kitchen chairs for them to sit on.

"Really, I should go. I don't want to intrude," Brooke said.

"Please stay?" Billy asked.

Logan was sure he made the plea in hopes the more gay people his parents saw, the better this talk might go. When Brooke looked to her for help, Logan simply shrugged. She took Brooke by the elbow and led her to the kitchen.

"Excuse us for just a moment, please," she said with a quick glance over her shoulder.

"Logan, I don't know these people," Brooke said when they were safely out of earshot. "I don't want to get involved with their family problems."

"Really? You've got a lot to learn if you're going to fit in with small town living." Logan gave her a grin. "All right, here's a quick rundown. Billy's thirty, and he still lives at home. I know, that's strange enough, right? I just found out a few days ago he's gay. He decided to tell his parents this evening, and it apparently didn't go well. They kicked him out, and he ended up here. Now I think you're up to speed, and you won't be completely lost once the conversation begins."

"Why does he want me here? This is something they should discuss in private, isn't it?"

"We're both gay," Logan said matter-of-factly. "He wants us in his corner, I guess. So will you stay?"

"Fine."

"Why did you come over anyway?"

"I already told you why I'm here. I'm sorry I got so upset with you the other night."

"See? You are attracted to me. I knew it." Logan couldn't help but smile and she was caught off guard by the rush of arousal she felt at the sight of Brooke's cheeks turning an irresistible shade of pink. She was only teasing, but was it possible the attraction she felt was mutual? Logan found herself hoping it was, but she walked away without giving Brooke an opportunity to respond.

Half an hour later, they were still in the living room talking. Very little progress had been made on Ray's part, but Logan could tell Missy didn't want to lose her son. She was trying hard to get Ray to compromise, but he wasn't budging. Logan, Brooke, and Jack had kept out of it until then, but Logan was done with the fly-on-the-wall routine.

"Ray, I understand you're scared, but he's your son. You can't possibly tell me this tiny bit of information changes things so drastically. He's not any different now than he was the last time you saw him, is he? You're like family to me, and you never turned your back on me when you found out I was gay."

"It's different when it isn't *your* child," Ray said, but he wouldn't look her in the eye as he spoke. "Your father had a hard time with it at first too. He and I talked about it a lot before he finally came to terms with it."

Logan sat back in her chair, her surprise at his words obviously apparent to the others in the room. Brooke put a hand on her knee and squeezed gently. Logan looked at Jack, who appeared as surprised as she was at the statement. Logan had always thought her father accepted her from the beginning. He'd never given any outward signs of struggling with it.

"He loved you, don't get me wrong, but he simply didn't understand how a fifteen-year-old kid could make that kind of declaration with such certainty," Ray said quietly. A wistful smile tugged at his lips. "Your mother never faltered though. You were her child, and she would have stood by your side no matter what. When all was said and done, all they ever wanted was for you to be happy, Logan."

"Think about what you just said, Ray," Logan said. "Apply it to your situation now. I never pictured you being one of those fathers who would disown their kid because he wasn't what you wanted him to be. All a parent should *ever* want is for their children to be safe, happy, and healthy. Nothing else should matter."

Logan looked down at her knee, where Brooke's hand was still resting. She took a chance and covered it with her own. Brooke didn't pull away as Logan had expected, but rather turned her hand over and allowed their fingers to intertwine. Logan tried to swallow the lump in her throat as emotions foreign to her welled up inside.

"You were incredible tonight, Logan," Brooke said after the Bests had gone home—all three of them—and Jack had gone upstairs to bed. They were standing in the foyer by the front door. "One minute you're the most annoying person I've ever met, and the next you show a soft and vulnerable side I'd never expect from you."

"I like to keep you guessing. If I showed you all of my good qualities up front, then there'd be no reason for you to stick around. There'd be no surprises down the road."

"Then you want me to stick around?"

"I definitely do," Logan whispered.

Brooke stared at Logan's lips, trying to keep her breathing even. God, she wanted to taste those lips again, but that would be bad, wouldn't it? She was having a hard time believing it would be anything but good.

She didn't pull away when Logan touched her cheek with just her fingertips. Logan tucked a strand of Brooke's hair behind her ear before dropping her hand back to her side. Brooke somehow managed to keep from begging her to touch her again.

"You're beautiful, Brooke." Logan's eyes turned a shade darker, causing Brooke's knees to go weak. "You have no idea how much I want to kiss you right now."

"Then why haven't you done it?" Brooke didn't recognize her own voice.

"Because I know I wouldn't be able to stop with just a kiss." Logan touched her face again, her thumb gently rubbing across her bottom lip. Brooke closed her eyes and sighed. "You have the most kissable lips I've ever seen."

"Do you have any idea what you're doing to me?" This was not good. So much for not wanting to let Logan know she was attracted to her.

"Hopefully the same thing you're doing to me."

Brooke met Logan's eyes as Logan leaned closer. The rush of excitement was palpable, and Brooke wanted to back away from her. Unfortunately, her body wasn't taking orders from her brain any longer. Her gaze dropped to Logan's mouth and she knew Logan was about to kiss her. Instead of protesting, she closed her eyes and waited for the first contact of those beautiful full lips. She waited, but it didn't come, and she felt an enormous amount of regret.

Logan was smiling at her, her green eyes almost black in the dim light of the foyer. Logan grabbed Brooke's hand, raised it to her lips, and placed a lingering kiss on her palm.

"Have dinner with me again."

"What?" Brooke asked, certain her confusion was obvious. "A date? You're seriously asking me on a date?"

"You sound surprised." Logan put a hand to her heart as though Brooke's words had truly wounded her.

"I'm sorry, but don't you remember our first date? It did not go well." Brooke pulled her hand away and finally took a step back. The distance seemed to bring some clarity to her fuzzy mind. "And you're certainly not the type I would date anyway."

"What just happened? We were about to kiss, weren't we?"

"But we didn't, did we?" Brooke knew her answer was evasive, but she didn't want to admit she'd had a moment of weakness. The uncertainty in Logan's eyes was almost enough to break through her resolve, but she reached for the doorknob before she could get sucked back in. "Good night, Logan."

"What about dinner?"

Brooke left without answering and didn't give in to the nagging thoughts in the back of her mind until she was in her own bedroom, the door shut firmly behind her. What had happened to the determination to never get involved again? Whether Brooke wanted to admit it or not, she *was* involved with Logan Swift. That was evident by how much Brooke wanted her—and by the amount of time Logan spent in her head. As she got under the covers knowing sleep wouldn't come easily, Brooke promised herself she would try to stay away from her.

CHAPTER SEVENTEEN

L ogan waited for Brooke to get in touch with her, but when a few days had passed with no contact, she couldn't stand it any longer. She knew the attraction between them was mutual—if it wasn't, Brooke never would have let them come so close to kissing the other night. Logan didn't like knowing she wanted more from Brooke than she ever had with any other woman, but she'd spent the days since their almost kiss coming to terms with what she was feeling.

She took a deep breath before ringing the doorbell and then quickly ran her fingers through her hair to try to make herself more presentable. When the door opened, she let out the breath she'd been holding.

"Hello, Logan," Henry said in his usual gruff tone. He backed the wheelchair up to allow Logan entry into the house. "What can I do for you?"

"I was actually looking for Brooke, Henry. Is she around?"

"Brooke!" he called as he wheeled himself back to the television and settled in again. "You have a visitor."

Logan tried to hold back the smile at the realization she was lucky she'd timed her visit with a commercial break. Logan took a moment to acknowledge the fact Henry didn't look well. He was pale, and she was about to ask him if he was all right when Brooke entered the room from the kitchen.

"What is it, Grandpa?" Brooke stopped short when she saw Logan, and her eyes flashed her irritation. "Hello, Logan."

"Can we talk for a moment? In private?"

"I don't think we have anything to talk about."

"On the contrary, we have plenty to talk about," Logan said with a nervous glance at Henry. She smiled politely and nodded once in Peggy's direction when she walked in behind Brooke.

"You can say whatever you have to say right here." It was obvious Brooke wasn't going to budge, so Logan sighed.

"Fine. I want you to go out to dinner with me. I'm sorry if I said or did anything the other night to make you angry, but I've been miserable the past couple of days. I feel like you're avoiding me." Logan said it all in a rush, afraid if she didn't then she would never get it out. She thought she saw something in Brooke's eyes to indicate a softening in her attitude toward dating her, but then crossed her arms over her chest.

"I said no the other night."

"Actually, you didn't come right out and say no," Logan said. "You said I'm not the type you would date. I'd like to change your mind about that assumption if you'd just give me the opportunity."

"I can't, Logan." Brooke took a look around the room and apparently decided the conversation would be better in private after all. Even her grandfather had focused his attention on them instead of the television. She motioned for Logan to follow her into the kitchen. "I told you how badly my breakup with Wendy hurt me. I don't *want* to date. Not you or anyone else. I'm sorry, but I just don't have it in me to try again."

Logan nodded as if she understood completely, but she didn't. It'd been close to a year since Brooke's relationship had ended. Logan would never do anything to hurt her, but there was no way she could convince her of it if Brooke wasn't even willing to try. Logan moved closer to her, placed a hand on Brooke's cheek, and leaned down to give her a chaste kiss on the lips.

"Honestly, I didn't think I had it in me either," she said, her voice barely above a whisper. "But then you walked into my life and turned everything upside down."

Brooke held her breath when Logan brushed her thumb across her lower lip before walking out of the kitchen. When she heard the front door close, Brooke angrily wiped the tear from her cheek. She couldn't get the heartrending look Logan had in her eyes before she left out of her head.

"Fuck," she muttered under her breath. If Logan was willing to try, why couldn't she? Then again, Logan could just be telling her what she wanted to hear in order to add another conquest to her list. Somehow the thought didn't quite jibe with the Logan she'd come to know. "Double fuck."

"Did you say something, dear?" her grandmother asked as she reentered the kitchen.

Brooke whirled around to face her, frantically going through her mind to figure out if she'd said it loud enough for her grandmother to hear. She relaxed when she remembered she'd been almost whispering.

"No, Gram, nothing," she said with a forced smile.

They went about finishing their cookie-baking marathon. It was less than two weeks until Christmas, and Marlene and Shane were due to arrive over the weekend. Brooke was just getting into what she was doing again when her grandmother reached over and pulled the rolling pin gently out of her hands.

"But—"

"The cookies can wait. Come sit with me a minute." She took Brooke's hand and led her to the table. Brooke sat and her grandmother went about getting them both a cup of hot apple cider before joining her. "Why did you turn down her request to join her for dinner?"

"Gram, I don't have it in me to date."

"Yes, I know what you told her, and maybe you even believe it yourself, but I see the way she looks at you, and the way *you* look at *her*." Her grandmother smiled in a way that could only be described as wistful, and Brooke chose not to be angry she'd just confessed to eavesdropping. "So what if you went out to dinner with her? It doesn't have to mean anything, does it? Spend some time getting to know her. If it's right, well, then you can deal with whatever feelings you might have. If it's not, then no harm done, right? But I'd think it would be better to know than to always wonder *what if?*"

"You make it sound so simple, Gram." She put a hand over her grandmother's and squeezed gently.

"Because it is. Young people today have no sense of romance. You go next door right now and tell her you'll go out with her while I finish up these cookies." Her grandmother walked over to the counter without waiting for a response, and Brooke simply smiled.

She was surprised when no one answered the door at Logan's, and a quick glance at the street confirmed Logan's car was gone. She shrugged and walked back to her grandparents' house. She'd just have to talk to her later.

❖

Logan walked into the club at close to eleven that night intent on getting drunk and forgetting about her problems. Billy was on call, so if a body needed to be picked up, he could do it on his own. She really needed to find a distraction for the night. Brooke's rejection earlier had stung more than Logan wanted to admit. She'd gone back to the funeral home and caught up on some paperwork before deciding to make the drive to Buffalo. She didn't need to chase after a woman who didn't want her. There were plenty who would gladly spend a bit of time with her. She nodded to the bartender to indicate she wanted her usual before taking a look around to see what her prospects were for the night.

The blonde playing pool looked like a possibility, but the woman she was playing against saw Logan watching her. The kiss they shared served to let Logan know the blonde wasn't available. She sighed and turned back around as the bartender, Stacy, set her shot of tequila in front of her.

"Keep them coming, Stacy," Logan said before running her tongue along the salt coating the rim of the glass. She downed the shot and winced at the burn that followed, but declined the offered slice of lime. After the first one, they always went down easier.

"Bad day?" Stacy asked with a laugh as she refilled the glass.

"Bad few weeks," Logan said with a nod. "My dad died a week before Thanksgiving. I haven't really been in the mood to go out since then."

"I'm sorry to hear it, Swift. Let me know if I can do anything."

"You can leave the bottle." Logan watched her walk away. Stacy was always nice to her, but she'd never given a thought to whether she might be interested in spending a little time getting to know each other better. She laughed when she noticed there was only enough left in the bottle for a couple more shots at best. Stacy turned and winked at her, and Logan felt it between her legs. "Shit."

She'd been coming to the bar long enough to know every bartender at least by name, and she knew a couple far better than that. She downed the second drink and turned to survey the dance floor. There were only three couples out there, and they all looked like they were madly in love. Logan sighed. She didn't get it. What was so great about love, anyway? Waking up next to the same woman day after day sounded pretty damn boring to her. And she sure as hell wouldn't be able to go out drinking and blowing off steam. No, love was overrated as far as she was concerned. You spend your lives together, and then one day it's gone. Better she remembered now than later. Death had a way of totally ruining everything. She'd seen it time and time again—the hopelessness and devastation of the people left behind. Jack might have thought he knew her reasons for avoiding love, but he could never truly get it.

But if she really still believed all of the things she'd been holding onto for so many years, then why was she experiencing feelings for Brooke? Because when all was said and done, she knew that much was true. Brooke had managed to get past her defenses as if they'd never existed at all. But Brooke made it perfectly clear she wasn't interested in Logan, and Logan wasn't about to beg for anything.

Shit. Her life was a bigger mess now than it had ever been when Julie broke up with her. It was Brooke she wanted, but here she was sitting in a bar two hours away from home—and for what? To pick up a faceless, nameless woman who could help put Brooke out of her mind? Logan wasn't completely sure forgetting her was even possible.

"Hey, Swift," Stacy said. Logan turned toward the voice when she felt a gentle hand on her forearm. "You aren't driving home tonight, are you?"

"You know I live almost two hours from here." She looked at her watch and was surprised to see it was after midnight. She was a little buzzed from her three shots, but nowhere near drunk. The bar usually stayed open until three, but on weeknights when there were no customers, the bartenders could close the place at their discretion. She'd finished the bottle Stacy left for her and was working on her second cup of coffee. As much as she wanted to drown her sorrows, those days were long gone for her. The mornings after weren't worth it as far as Logan was concerned.

"You have a place to stay?"

Logan shook her head and felt her pulse quicken. This was the dance she was used to. Maybe this was all she needed. A quick romp with someone to take the edge off, because maybe all she was feeling for Brooke was lust and not really…something else.

Fat chance.

"I was going to get a room at the motel on the edge of town."

"You could do that," she said as Logan watched her fingers move slowly up her arm until they stopped at her elbow. Stacy leaned in so her mouth was close enough to Logan's ear for her to feel the warm breath. "Or you could come home with me for the night. If you're feeling up to it."

"You're sure you wouldn't mind?" Logan's mouth was dry.

"I'll be ready to leave in about ten minutes. Help yourself to some more coffee." Stacy disappeared into the office off the end of the bar.

Logan pulled her phone out of her pocket and thought briefly about calling Jack but decided it might do him some good to wonder where she was all night. She chuckled and admitted to herself he probably wouldn't even notice she wasn't there. She shoved the phone back into her pocket before heading to the bathroom to splash some cold water on her face.

Logan was taken aback by Stacy's aggressiveness. The second the door to her apartment closed, she had Logan pinned against it. Logan turned her head when Stacy moved in to kiss her, and in one smooth move, reversed their positions. Logan wasn't comfortable not being in control. Stacy threaded her arms around Logan's neck, pulling her closer as their mouths collided. Stacy moaned when Logan's hand moved under her shirt and up her side to cup her breast. She pulled Stacy's shirt up and over her head, then held her hands there with one of her own while she reached behind and unclasped Stacy's bra with the other.

She had the fleeting thought she shouldn't be doing this if she ever hoped to have a chance with Brooke, but then again, Brooke had made it clear she wasn't interested in her. She forced herself to focus on the body in front of her and not the body she couldn't have.

Logan took a nipple in her mouth and was a little surprised by the intensity of Stacy's reaction. She began writhing beneath her until Logan placed a thigh firmly between her legs. Logan's teeth scraped across the nipple and she moaned when she felt the heat through both of their jeans. Logan let go of her arms and moved up to kiss her neck. Stacy's arms went around her and she held on tight as she moved quicker and quicker against Logan's leg, her breath coming in short gasps. Logan couldn't do anything but hold on when Stacy's orgasm started. She bucked against Logan violently and screamed out her pleasure.

Logan buried her face in her neck, breathing in her scent.

"You smell so damn good, Brooke," she said. She stiffened and sucked in a breath when the words registered, but Stacy was still panting and pressing hard against her thigh. Logan pulled back to look at her, but Stacy just smiled, her eyes hooded and her lips swollen.

"I'll be whoever you want me to be, sugar, but don't you dare stop touching me."

Logan took a step away and helped Stacy steady herself. *Who the hell doesn't care when the person they're having sex with calls them by someone else's name?* Logan couldn't remember ever even using anyone's name in the heat of the moment before. It was easier because then she didn't have to try to recall the woman's name at all. She tried to think of *anything* other than the throbbing between her legs. The throbbing she wanted Brooke to take care of for her.

She breathed a sigh of relief when her phone rang and she began searching pockets until she found it. At least she still had all her clothes on. Stacy grabbed the phone away from her and shook her head.

"Your turn now," she said. She began walking backward down the hallway, and Logan had no choice but to follow. She had her phone in her hand. All Logan had been able to see before it was snatched away from her was Jack's name. "Take your clothes off, Swift."

"Give me the phone, Stacy." Logan was in no mood to play games, and she was certain her tone conveyed her urgency. "No one would call this late unless there was an emergency."

Stacy stopped just inside the bedroom and handed it to her, pouting. She went and got a T-shirt to put on while Logan sat on the edge of the bed and started to dial Jack's number. She wasn't even halfway through when the phone chimed, indicating a text message.

Where the hell r u? Call me!

She finished dialing and Jack answered on the first ring.

"Jesus, Logan—"

"What's wrong? Why are you calling so late?"

"Henry's had a stroke," Jack said, sounding a little unnerved. "The ambulance took him to Saint Vincent Health Center in Erie."

"Is he all right?" Logan was trying not to panic. First her father and now this? Hadn't there been enough death this holiday season? She reminded herself it was a stroke. A stroke didn't necessarily mean death. People had strokes all the time, right?

"What's wrong?" Stacy asked when Logan stood and headed toward the front door.

Logan asked Jack to hold on and took the phone from her ear. She turned back to Stacy. "I'm sorry, but I need to get home. Family emergency. Thanks for everything." Logan was struck by the pissed off look on Stacy's face, but she couldn't deal with a fragile ego now. She had to get to the hospital twenty minutes ago. She turned without another word and ran out to her car. "Jack, how's he doing?"

"It's not looking too good, to be perfectly honest. Peggy rode in the ambulance with Henry and Brooke followed them to the hospital. Come pick me up so we can be there for them. I don't think they're going to take it well if he doesn't make it."

"That might be a bit difficult, Jack. I'm in Buffalo. I can be at the hospital in about ninety minutes."

"What the hell are you doing in Buffalo? Jesus, Logan, where is the hospital? I'll be able to get there a lot sooner than you."

"Twenty-fifth street between Myrtle and Sassafras. Tell Peggy I'll be there as soon as I can."

Logan disconnected and tossed the phone onto the passenger seat before speeding up to merge onto the Interstate. With little to no traffic on the roads, she could make it there in less than an hour. If it was time for Henry to go, she knew Peggy would deal with it better than anyone thought she would. It was Brooke Logan was worried about. She wanted to be there for her, and nothing was going to stop her.

CHAPTER EIGHTEEN

Logan entered the emergency room an hour and ten minutes after she'd hung up with Jack. She was pretty sure she'd managed to break almost every traffic law on the books, but luck had been on her side—especially since it started to snow pretty heavily halfway there. She ran through the automatic doors and went straight to triage where she wasn't happy to find Gretchen on duty.

"Hey, Tiger, what brings you here so early on a snowy morning?" Gretchen asked when she saw her coming toward the desk. The grin indicated Gretchen was happy to see her, even though their last meeting hadn't gone well. "I don't remember calling for a body to be picked up."

"I don't have time for niceties right now, Gretchen. I need to know where Henry Collier is. He would have been brought in about an hour ago, give or take. My brother told me he had a stroke."

"Family only, sweetie," she said after looking it up on the computer in front of her. "Sorry, but I can't let you go up."

"Come on, Gretchen, he *is* family." Logan looked around the waiting room for Jack but didn't see him anywhere. There were less people there than she would have thought at that time of morning. She turned back to Gretchen. "I don't see my brother here, so you must have let him up, didn't you?"

"The doctor did. He's a fan." Gretchen rolled her eyes. Just one of the strikes against her—she didn't like football. Gretchen leaned across the counter and grabbed Logan by the shirtfront before pulling her closer. "Promise to go out with me this weekend and I'll let you go up."

"Seriously? Blackmail when I'm worried about someone I love?" Logan grabbed her wrist and twisted it hard enough to make Gretchen let go, but not so hard she cried out. She did her best to keep her voice down, but it was a losing battle. "Are you really telling me I can't get in to see the man who's like a grandfather to me unless I promise to fuck you?"

"Logan?"

She turned to see Jack emerging from the elevator and she walked quickly toward him after giving Gretchen a prolonged glare. She swore to herself she'd never see Gretchen again outside of a work setting. And if she did happen to run into her somewhere, she would turn right around and walk out again.

"Come upstairs with me," Jack said as he grabbed her by the arm and pulled her onto the waiting elevator. The doors closed before Jack spoke again. "What the hell was that all about?"

"I'll tell you later."

"Peggy's been asking why you aren't here. Are you going to tell me why the hell you were in Buffalo, or do I have to wait until later for that too? Or maybe you don't need to tell me. I can smell the alcohol on your breath."

"I went for a drive. I needed to clear my head and there's a good gay bar there." It wasn't a complete lie, but Jack gave her one of those looks that said he thought she was full of shit but he wasn't going to press her about it. He pulled a tin of Altoids from his pocket and gave her one. "How's Brooke?"

"She's trying to stay strong for Peggy, but I can tell she's pretty upset." Jack looked up at the numbers corresponding to the floors they were passing before shifting his focus to his feet. "He probably isn't going to make it, Logan."

"It's that bad?"

"The doctor said it was a hemorrhagic stroke caused by a ruptured aneurysm."

"Shit." She followed Jack down a hallway to the ICU waiting room. "Was it in the brain stem?"

"Yes."

"But he's still alive, so that's a good sign." Logan came around the corner and saw Brooke holding Peggy. Her heart lurched with the probability Henry had already passed on. She rushed to Peggy's side.

"Oh, Logan, thank God you're here," Peggy said, standing and throwing her arms around Logan's waist where she held on to her tightly.

"What the hell are *you* doing here?" Brooke asked.

Logan looked over at her and felt a sudden wave of sadness when she recognized the irrational fear in Brooke's eyes. It was a look she'd seen many times from friends who had loved ones in the hospital.

"Peggy wanted me here."

"You're wrong. *We* don't want you here."

"Brooke," Jack said in a futile attempt to calm her down. Brooke stood and pulled away from him when he reached out to her.

"No, Jack, it's all right. I'll go," Logan said. Never mind she was about to suffer another loss in her life. She swallowed the lump in her throat and extricated herself from Peggy's grasp, but Peggy grabbed her hand before she could back away and refused to let go.

"You aren't going anywhere," Peggy said sternly before turning her attention to Brooke. "*You* may not want her here, Brooke, but I sure as hell do. And so would your grandfather. She's family to us."

Brooke never took her eyes off Logan while Logan finally got her hand out of Peggy's vice-like grip. Brooke was obviously upset with her, and Logan knew this wasn't a conversation to have in front of the wife of a possibly terminal patient. She assured Peggy she would stay if it was what she really wanted, but then Logan took Brooke by the elbow and led her down the hall back toward the bank of elevators.

"Brooke, I understand your fear, I really do," Logan began in the calmest voice she could manage. She took a deep breath and tried to put a cap on her emotions. Brooke was going to have enough to deal with without Logan breaking down too.

"How can you possibly understand?" Brooke asked with venom in her voice.

"This isn't the first time I've had someone freak out at me when I've shown up at the hospital to visit a patient."

"I really don't care about what you've dealt with in the past. I want you out of here. *He* doesn't want to see you." Brooke took a step back with a horrified look on her face. "Have you been drinking?"

"I had a couple of drinks, yes, but I promise you I'm not drunk."

"Why *did* it take you so long to get here, Logan? Were you in Buffalo, or Pittsburgh? I bet if I got close enough to you I'd smell sex too, wouldn't I? Leave. Just go home. I can't deal with this right now. He's still alive so we don't need you here."

Logan felt her heart break a little at the hurt and rejection in Brooke's expression and her tone. She couldn't think about any of it now. Henry and Peggy were the only people who mattered. They didn't need to deal with whatever shit was happening between her and their granddaughter.

"Brooke, I take care of the dead, I don't *cause* their deaths. I know if you would simply think about this in a rational way you'd see my being here isn't going to make him worse, nor is it going to make him better. I'm just a family friend who wants to be here for Peggy. She needs everyone by her side right now."

Brooke stared at her for a moment before giving her a curt nod and going back to Peggy. Logan didn't know if there would be any kind of an apology down the road or not, but she didn't really need one. It was merely the way some people dealt with the fear of losing a loved one. Logan hadn't been to visit anyone in the hospital in over five years because of the irrational fear people seemed to have with an undertaker being in the hospital. But this was Henry. She wasn't about to let Peggy go through this without her.

❖

Brooke was grateful Logan chose to sit on the other side of the room. She felt like an ass for reacting the way she had, but her stress levels had gone up exponentially in the past few hours. All she could see when Logan entered the waiting room was the funeral director part of her coming to collect her grandfather's body. Deep down she knew her fear was irrational, but the knowledge of it didn't change anything. She'd owe Logan an apology, but not now. She closed her eyes and rested her head against the wall.

"Mrs. Collier?" the doctor said, his voice waking Brooke up from her doze.

Brooke quickly rubbed her face and stood to help her grandmother to her feet. The doctor looked at Brooke with a sympathetic smile that caused a hitch in her breathing. She knew the look well. She knew what he was about to say and she didn't want to hear it. She didn't want her grandmother to hear it either, but there was nothing she could do to shield her from the news. That look was something she was sure they taught doctors in medical school because she'd seen it way too often in her time as a nurse in Philadelphia.

"Is Henry awake now? Can I go see him?" her grandmother asked, her tone hopeful. Brooke could see she was fighting back tears though, and she put her arm around her grandmother in an attempt to comfort her.

Brooke breathed a sigh of relief when Logan and Jack came to stand on either side of them. Maybe it was a good thing to have these people so entrenched in her grandparents' lives. She should probably make an effort to be nicer to Logan because she was going to need all the help she could get in guiding her grandmother through this.

"I'm very sorry, Mrs. Collier, we did everything we could for your husband," the doctor said, his eyes darting back and forth between the four of them. "The fact is his brain was simply denied oxygen for too long. As you know, he was unresponsive when he arrived here at the hospital, and unfortunately, we weren't able to bring him back."

"No, he can't be gone," her grandmother said, her tone brusque. She tried to push past him, but Logan was there with a hand to stop her. Her grandmother turned and looked at her. "He can't be gone, Logan, he has a doctor's appointment tomorrow." Her eyes went wide and she clutched Logan's arm tightly. The tears came as the realization of the doctor's words seemed to finally register. "I didn't get a chance to tell him good-bye. I need to tell him how much I love him."

"I'm sure he knows how much you love him, Peggy," Logan said gently as she put a hand on the side of her head and encouraged her grandmother to lean on her. Brooke watched with interest as Logan held her grandmother and encouraged her to cry, to let it all out. There was a part of her that wished Logan would hold and comfort her too. Logan spared a glance for the doctor.

"I'm so sorry, Logan," he said, sounding as though he truly meant it. Perhaps the doctor knew of the loss Logan had already suffered. "Will you be handling this, or should I send a nurse out to get the information?"

"We're good. I'll take care of it all."

The doctor walked away and her grandmother continued to cry and buried her face in Logan's chest. Logan held her for a few moments before helping her into a waiting room chair. Brooke sat in the chair next to her and held her grandmother's hand.

"Jack," Logan said quietly. Jack was at her side in an instant. "Do me a favor and give Billy a call. He knows what to do."

Brooke was grateful her grandfather had made his own funeral arrangements because she knew she wouldn't be able to take care of it. And she knew without a doubt there was no way her grandmother could deal with it. Nothing in her training as a nurse had prepared her for the loss of a loved one. It was one thing to comfort the family of someone who'd died, but quite another to deal with the loss yourself. She stayed with her grandmother until Jack returned from making his phone call. Brooke stood and motioned for Logan to follow her, and Jack moved closer to her grandmother. She moved them far enough away so they could speak without being overheard.

"She's in no condition to deal with any funeral arrangements."

"There's no need. They've already planned everything. Neither one of you will have to do a thing other than show up for the funeral."

"Thank you, Logan. You were amazing with her just now." Brooke could feel the tears welling up inside her. The last thing she needed right then was to allow Logan to see her so vulnerable. "I'm sorry about how I reacted earlier."

"There's no need for an apology," Logan said with a quick glance over her shoulder. "Stress can do crazy things to people sometimes."

"It's no excuse for the way I behaved, but saying I'm sorry doesn't seem like enough to me." Brooke grabbed Logan's arm but quickly pulled away again when she felt a wave of dizziness.

Brooke found it impossible to hold in her emotions any longer. When the tears started flowing, Logan wrapped her arms around her, and Brooke didn't have the strength to resist her. She allowed Logan to hold her as she cried. Neither of them said anything, and Brooke was sure she felt Logan's tears as well as her own. After what felt like forever, Brooke finally took a step back and wiped away the tears.

"I feel like I need to make it up to you somehow."

"Have dinner with me again."

Brooke was surprised by Logan's request, not because of the timing, but because she looked so serious. It was apparent Logan was slightly taken aback as well. Brooke found herself smiling through her tears.

"I'm sorry. That was very inappropriate," Logan said and shoved her hands in her pockets.

"Then you don't want to have dinner with me?"

"Yes. I mean no. I mean…" Logan sighed in obvious frustration. "I would love to have dinner with you, Brooke. I think you know that, but this wasn't the right time to ask you out. Please forgive me."

"We went out once, and it ended badly." Brooke knew she didn't really need to remind Logan of it. She closed her eyes and tried to remember exactly how bad it ended, but all she could picture was the two of them kissing. "And then when you finally got up the nerve to ask me again, I kind of put you in your place, didn't I?"

"I'm sure I deserved it."

"So…you're really asking me on another date?" Brooke thought the shade of red Logan's face turned was adorable.

"It can be a date, if that's what you want, or it could simply be two friends having dinner together."

"Which do you want it to be?"

"A date," Logan said without hesitation. "Definitely a date."

CHAPTER NINETEEN

They decided it would be better to wait until after the funeral to go on their date because they agreed it might be hard for her grandmother to see them enjoying themselves while she was still mourning the loss of her husband.

Brooke had been trying to get in touch with her father ever since the night her grandfather had died, but no one ever answered her calls until now. Her parents were still living in the Philadelphia area so she knew they'd have time to make it for the funeral if they wanted to. She really hadn't wanted to leave a message about his death, so she kept calling, figuring if she didn't connect before the funeral, *then* she would leave a message. When her father finally answered the phone, she sighed in frustration when he reacted the way she already knew he would.

"I said I'm not coming to the funeral. I told you they were dead because they are, at least to me. The fact he really has died doesn't change anything for me, Brooke."

"Dad, I really wish you'd reconsider. Grandma needs her family now more than ever. He's gone. Can't you see past your anger enough to let it go?"

"No, and I'm not discussing this anymore. If you really cared about him, then I truly am sorry for your loss, Brooke, but I stopped caring about either one of them long before you were even born."

"What happened to tear this family apart so thoroughly?" Brooke knew he wouldn't tell her because he never had before, and this was far from the first time she'd asked about it.

"Ask your grandmother, though I doubt she'll tell you the truth. I need to go. I'm working the night shift this week. I love you."

He hung up before she had the chance to respond. She fought the urge to throw the phone across the kitchen and turned to find her grandmother waiting in the doorway.

"That was your father," she said—a statement, not a question. Her eyes were as cold and distant as her tone. Without waiting for any kind of confirmation, she poured herself a cup of coffee and took a seat at the kitchen table. "Is he coming to the funeral?"

"He refuses, Gram. I wish someone would tell me why things are so bad between you and him. When I was growing up, he told me his parents were dead."

If Brooke's revelation surprised her, she never showed any outward sign of it. Brooke watched in silence while she sipped her coffee at the ancient table she'd probably had for decades. After what seemed an eternity, her grandmother leaned back in her chair and motioned for Brooke to take a seat across from her.

"Is it really so bad you can't see your way past it and forgive him? Maybe if you called him he'd talk to you."

"It's not about me forgiving him, dear." Her grandmother rearranged the flowers sitting in the middle of the table. "It's about him forgiving me, and I know it will never happen."

Brooke sat back and folded her arms across her chest, deciding she wasn't going to move from her chair until her grandmother told her the whole story. To her surprise, she didn't have to wait long.

"Your father was a hell-raiser and a troublemaker from the time he was old enough to walk," she said quietly.

Despite the harshness of her words, Brooke caught the undercurrent of affection in her tone. Her grandmother stared at some point on the wall behind Brooke. Brooke had the feeling she was calling forth old memories. She just hoped they weren't too painful for her grandmother because she had enough to deal with.

"His first scrape with the law came when he was twelve. He and a friend stole a bottle of whiskey from the friend's father's liquor cabinet and proceeded to drink themselves into a stupor. The police picked him up and brought him home. We were told if it happened again we'd be getting a call telling us he was in jail. Your grandfather was livid, Brooke. We grounded him for a year after that, but nothing was going to stop him. By the time he turned fifteen, he'd been arrested seven times. Four of them were for drunk driving. We kept bailing him out and paying for lawyers to defend him, and he swore to us he'd never do anything wrong again. He always did though. We were at our wit's end. We even sent him away to a boarding school for troubled boys, but he got expelled before the year was out."

"Jesus, how bad do you have to be to get kicked out of a school for troubled boys?" Brooke was reeling after learning these things about her father. He'd told her about an idyllic childhood. Of course, she'd learned that much wasn't true when she'd found her grandparents. Once she knew they were alive, his story changed, and Brooke was told they'd been horrible parents and he didn't want anything to do with them. "I'm sorry I interrupted you, Gram, please go on."

When her grandmother failed to say anything for a long moment, Brooke was worried she wasn't going to get the rest of the story after all. Her grandmother continued to move the spoon on the table a millimeter to the left, and then back again. When she started talking again, her voice sounded trapped in the past, quiet and lost.

"When he was seventeen, he was arrested for raping a fifteen-year-old girl. Your grandfather and I agonized for days over what to do about him. We finally decided we were done helping him because it was obvious we were only making it possible for him to get more and more out of control. Who knows? If we'd bailed him out, the next time it might have been murder." Her grandmother looked at Brooke then and wiped her eyes. "He was tried as an adult and was convicted. He spent ten years in prison. The only time we ever heard from him was the day you were born. He got our number by calling information, and he only called us to let us know we had a granddaughter we'd never have the opportunity to get to know. You were born three years before he was released from prison."

"How..." Brooke started, but she didn't even know what question to ask. Her mother told her she'd met her father at a concert when they were both twenty-two. But the story her grandmother was telling put him in prison until he was twenty-seven. She shook her head.

"Your grandfather had a friend do some investigating and we found out your mother was one of those women who sympathizes with prisoners and started writing to your father in jail. After they corresponded through the mail for a couple of years, she finally went to visit him. From what I understand, they were married for a few months before you were conceived. She apparently wasn't using her real name when she went to visit him because there's no record of her outside the prison. When your father was released, it was as if they fell off the face of the earth. We wanted more than anything to find you and get you away from them, Brooke. We knew there was no way they'd give you a stable upbringing. But we couldn't find you."

Her father was a convicted rapist. Brooke really didn't know how to process the information. They drank too much, yes, but there was never any doubt both her parents loved her dearly. It certainly hadn't been an ideal childhood, yet she'd never wanted for anything.

The grim reality took hold. Her entire life had been a lie. Nothing about her parents' pasts were real—at least not the pasts they'd talked about with her. Brooke felt dizzy and was afraid she might pass out.

"Marlene never told me any of this," Brooke said.

"Why would she?" her grandmother asked. "She was only six when he went to prison, and we never talked about it around her. All she knew was what happened between us and her brother was so bad it could never be fixed. We never saw the need to tell her about the things he'd done, and eventually, she pretty much forgot about him. It wasn't like we ever went to visit him in prison. She only found him when she came across your name in admissions at Temple. And I'm so happy she did."

"Logan said she never knew you had a son." Brooke was stunned and she knew it was obvious in the way her voice shook when she spoke.

"We moved here a year after he was arrested. Before then, we were living near Harrisburg. We had to get away from the people who knew what he'd done." Her grandmother was staring at her hands but finally tore her gaze away to look at Brooke again. "We needed a fresh start. We wanted to raise Marlene in an environment where she wouldn't be ostracized simply because of something her brother had done. No one in Oakville knows anything about your father."

Brooke stood without another word and made her way to the front porch. She was dazed, there was no denying that. She felt like she should be incredibly angry upon hearing the truth about her father, but the rug had been pulled out from under her and her whole world was askew. She was glad he refused to come to the funeral. She really didn't think she could face him right now. Not after everything she'd learned.

"Hey, Brooke," Jack said when he came out the front door. Brooke apparently looked like she needed a shoulder to cry on because he came to sit next to her, concern etched in his face. "Are you all right?"

"Just family bullshit."

"Listen, I'm meeting Logan for a couple of drinks. Come with me. It'll help you relax."

"Marlene's going to be here soon, and I really shouldn't leave my grandmother alone." Brooke wanted to go, but she knew running away from the things she'd been told about her family wouldn't help anything. Then again, maybe some mindless drinking could help her forget about all the lies she'd been told while growing up. But did she really want to see Logan when she was so raw? She didn't have to think about it for long. Logan was the one person she wanted to see.

"Peggy can take care of herself until Marlene gets here." Jack nudged her with his shoulder and she couldn't help laughing. His grin was contagious. "Come on, you know you want to go."

"Okay." She finally relented, already looking forward to seeing Logan. "Give me a minute to grab a jacket."

❖

"Where are you?" Jack asked loud enough so Logan had to pull the phone away from her ear. "I'm already a couple drinks up on you, so you'd better hurry."

"How many women are buying you drinks?" Logan asked as she locked her door and headed for the entrance to the only bar within twelve miles of their home. It was a halfway decent place, although Logan would have preferred a restaurant in Riverside or even Erie over the dive Jack suggested.

"Aside from the fact Cynthia wouldn't be happy about it, I don't think anybody in this place even knows who I am."

He sounded a little stunned by the revelation, and Logan laughed as she entered the place. She saw him sitting at the corner of the bar and put her phone away without responding as she walked up behind him.

"I highly doubt that, brother," she said with a hearty clap to his shoulder. "You're like a god around here."

"Yeah, well, nobody's said anything. Not even the bartender. She's kind of cute, but she seems more interested in Brooke than me."

"Brooke's here?" Logan was taken aback at the rush of arousal she experienced at just the mere thought she was actually there. Ever since the night in the hospital when Brooke had agreed to have dinner with her, she'd been all Logan could think about. She scanned the room and stopped when she saw Brooke. The bartender was indeed interested in her, and Logan felt a pang of what could only be jealousy. She didn't like the feeling, and it was appearing more and more where Brooke was concerned. Jealous meant you cared enough about someone to experience the feeling, and she never cared about anyone that much. At least not until now. "Why is she here?"

"She was dealing with some *family bullshit*," he said. When Logan looked at him, he shrugged. "Her words, not mine. She looked a little down, so I invited her along. You don't mind, do you?"

"Why would I mind?" Logan asked with more bravado than she felt. "She certainly doesn't look like she's down now."

"She's been chatting up the bartender for quite some time."

Logan felt her ears burning, and she knew Jack was watching her watching Brooke. She forced herself to pull her gaze away from the two women and looked at him, one eyebrow raised in question. She hadn't told him about the date she and Brooke had yet to plan because she knew he'd tease her about it. She wasn't about to give him the satisfaction of knowing he was right about the attraction between them now.

"Are you jealous?" he asked with a smirk.

"Of what? We're friends, Jack." She waved a hand in dismissal and turned her back on them. She took a deep breath to try to calm her thundering heart. She grabbed Jack's beer and downed half of it in one gulp.

"Except for the fact you both want each other. But you go right ahead and keep telling yourself you're just friends, because I, for one, don't believe a word of it." Jack laughed and turned his attention to the sports news show on the television behind the bar.

Logan clenched her fists to keep herself from slapping him in the back of the head.

CHAPTER TWENTY

Logan placed the cooler beside her chair and took a seat on the front porch. She'd stayed at the bar long enough to have one beer with Jack. Then she'd left him with the directive to not leave without making sure Brooke had a way to get home, since Brooke hadn't left her conversation with the bartender the whole time she was there. He'd laughed at her. She couldn't explain to him yet the way she was feeling about Brooke, and him laughing at her really rubbed her the wrong way.

She unscrewed the cap from her first bottle of beer just as the front door opened on the Colliers' side of the porch. Logan smiled when she saw Shane, Marlene's fifteen-year-old son emerge. He'd been ten the first time she'd met him. He'd been sitting on the front porch with her father drinking a root beer while her father drank a real beer. The kid was older than his years, and they'd had some pretty deep discussions.

"Hey, Shane," she said. He turned to look at her with a weary smile.

"Hey, Swift," he said.

Logan reached into the cooler and pulled out a bottle of the root beer she'd picked up on the way home from the bar. She knew Shane would be there and wanted to be prepared. He stepped over the railing and took it from her as he collapsed into the other chair with a sigh. They sat in comfortable silence watching the light snow falling.

"How are you holding up?" she asked after a few minutes.

"I'll be okay," he said before taking a swig. He turned his attention to her and she looked away quickly. She didn't want him to see how sad she was. He had enough to deal with. "I didn't get to see you over Thanksgiving. I'm really sorry about your dad. How are you?"

"I'll be okay."

"I really liked him. He never treated me like a kid, you know?" Shane sat back and took another drink from the brown bottle. Her dad had always given him the bottles so he'd feel more like an adult. "You never did either. Not like some people do."

"You never acted like a kid, Shane. I'm not sure I believe you're only fifteen." Logan grinned when he laughed. They were silent again, and as the silence went on, Logan couldn't stop her mind from wandering to Brooke. "How come you never told me about your cousin Brooke?"

"I don't know." He shrugged and stared at the bottle as he turned it over and over in his hands. "She had a really bad breakup with her girlfriend earlier this year."

"She told me a little about it. How do you know about it?"

"I listen. People tend to forget there's a kid around when you spend more time listening than talking. I overheard a lot of phone conversations between my mom and Brooke." Shane cocked his head as he looked at her with a lopsided grin. "Do you like her?"

"I don't really know her very well." That wasn't entirely true. She knew *enough* about her. She was obviously a family oriented person, just like Logan. She also knew she cared deeply for her, but it wasn't something she intended to share with Shane. "I've only known her a little over a month."

"She's worth getting to know. She's been spending a lot of time with us since my dad died."

Logan felt tears welling up at the mention of Shane's father's death. He'd died only six months earlier, and Marlene had asked Logan and her father to try to help Shane through the loss. He'd only been fifty when cancer took his life. They hadn't even known about the cancer until three months before the end. It had been hard for Shane to understand, and Logan expected it was even harder for Marlene to move on. But they both seemed to be doing well now, which made Logan happy. It made her inexplicably pleased to think Brooke had helped them get to where they were now.

Logan couldn't stop her smile when she noticed Brooke's car pull up in front of the house. But nothing could have prepared her for the tirade she was about to face.

"Logan? What the hell?" she asked as she stormed up the steps. She looked at Shane and the bottle he held in his hand before refocusing on Logan. "Do you have any idea how old he is?"

"Of course I do." It was all Logan managed to get out before Brooke started again.

"Really? You know he's fifteen, yet here he is sharing a beer with you? How irresponsible can you be?"

Logan placed her bottle on the ground next to her chair before standing to face Brooke. She knew it looked like she was trying to intimidate her, but damn it, she hadn't done anything wrong, and she wasn't about to let Brooke rake her over the coals for nothing.

"Logan," Shane pleaded, but Logan ignored him, instead focusing her energy on Brooke.

"Yes, *I'm* drinking a beer," Logan said, the calm tone of her voice in stark contradiction to the anger she felt rising. How dare Brooke think she would give Shane a beer? "However, he's drinking a *root* beer. Take a sip if you don't believe me."

Brooke stared at her for a moment, and Logan could see the turmoil going on in her eyes. Brooke never broke their eye contact as she reached for the bottle, which Shane handed to her before storming off to the house next door.

"You know the difference between you and my mother, Brooke?" Shane asked before going inside. "My mother trusts me."

Logan couldn't help the smile tugging at the corners of her mouth at the thinly veiled jab, but when she saw the fire ignite in Brooke's eyes, she regretted it. Brooke slammed the bottle down on the railing without tasting it.

"What this is doesn't matter. What matters is it's almost eleven o'clock at night, and you're out here drinking with a minor."

Logan had enough. She walked into the house, but before she could shut the door behind her, Brooke forced her way inside.

"Don't walk away from me when I'm talking to you," she said.

Logan stopped in the doorway to the kitchen. When she turned to face Brooke, she wasn't prepared for the feelings welling up inside her. Brooke kept ranting, but Logan couldn't hear a word of it over the pulse pounding in her ears. Her breathing quickened, and before she knew what she was doing, she had Brooke pressed up against the wall. She was still talking when Logan covered her mouth with her own. Brooke let out a whimper and Logan pressed her body more firmly against her.

Logan's need ratcheted up a notch when Brooke's tongue slid along her lips, and her arms went around Logan's neck, pulling her closer. Logan grabbed her wrists and raised Brooke's arms above her head while pressing tighter against her body.

"What the hell do you think you're doing?" Brooke asked when she turned her head and broke the kiss. Logan moved her mouth to Brooke's neck, and Brooke rested her head against the wall, giving Logan better access.

"It was the only way I could think of to get you to shut up for half a second," Logan murmured against her skin. "You're beautiful when you're pissed off, do you know that?"

"I'm beginning to think you piss me off on purpose."

Logan laughed as she took a step back and ran a hand through her hair. She didn't even try to hide the fact she was breathing heavily, and she could see by the way Brooke's chest was rising and falling she was having the same dilemma. She wanted Brooke, and she wasn't interested in trying to hide the fact any longer.

"You're even more wound up than usual tonight," Logan said. "Is everything okay?"

"No, it isn't. I found out this afternoon my father is a convicted rapist, and the reason you know nothing about him is my grandparents moved here a year into his ten-year stint in prison."

"I'm sorry you had to find out the way you did. Is there anything I can do to help?" Logan knew it sounded ridiculous, but she didn't know what else to say.

"Hold me?"

The pain Logan saw in Brooke's eyes nearly melted her insides. She opened her arms and Brooke's body molded to hers perfectly.

"Stay the night with me." Logan knew the words came out wrong when Brooke pushed her away.

"Does everything come back to sex for you?"

"The offer has absolutely nothing to do with sex, I swear. I only wanted to offer a shoulder to cry on."

"I don't want to sleep with you."

Logan looked at her, not quite sure she'd heard her correctly. What did it mean when right after she'd assured Brooke it wasn't about sex, Brooke made a comment about sleeping with her? Perhaps everything came back to sex for Brooke.

"I think you do."

"What?" Brooke laughed, and Logan cringed at the reaction.

"Come on, the kiss, the way your body responds to me. I *know* you want to sleep with me," Logan said. "I guess I just need to work a little harder at convincing you."

A car door slammed outside and they both froze, waiting to determine whether it was Jack returning home. They heard footsteps coming up the walkway, but then someone entered the house next door. Once everything was silent again, they turned back to each other.

"Just for argument's sake," Brooke said, wondering how she'd managed to let this happen. Logan had a way of getting around her defenses like no one else had ever done. It seemed the madder she got, the more she was attracted to Logan. "If we did sleep together, what happens the next day?"

"What?" Logan seemed genuinely perplexed. "What do you mean?"

"If I slept with you, you'd probably never want to see me again, right? I've known women like you, Logan. I'm not cut out for casual. And I don't want to get close to someone just to have them dump me for some other woman."

"Why can't we just see where it goes? Who says it has to be casual? Or even long-term for that matter. We like each other, right?"

Brooke wanted to tell her she was wrong. She wanted to tell Logan she didn't like her at all, but she would be lying. Instead she said nothing. Logan apparently took her silence as a denial.

"Okay, fine," Logan said, her irritation showing in her stance. "Did you get Darcy's phone number? Have fun with her, Brooke, because she's the epitome of casual."

Brooke clenched her fists and took a deep breath. Of course Logan knew the bartender from the dive they were at earlier. Brooke

hadn't known Logan was there until well after she'd left. She'd
wanted to see Logan earlier in the bar. It was the reason she'd even
agreed to go with Jack in the first place. She'd desperately wanted
to share with her the things she'd learned about her father. The fact
Logan hadn't even bothered to say hi to her made her angrier still.

Yes, she *had* gotten Darcy's number, but Brooke had no intention
of ever calling her. Hell, she'd only sat there talking to Darcy for so
long because she didn't want to come across as being rude. It was
Logan she'd wanted to see. As much as she didn't want to admit it,
she was pretty damn sure she was falling for Logan, and there wasn't
anything she could do about it.

"Really? You don't get what you want so you tear down someone
else?"

"You aren't into casual, so I just wanted to warn you," Logan
said with a shrug. "I'm speaking from experience on this one."

"If you're so concerned about it, why didn't you talk to me at the
bar? Why let her try and charm her way into my pants?"

"Because I knew you'd shut her down just like you're doing with
me. And if not, well, that's not my business."

"God, you are so infuriating." Brooke took a step toward her.
When Logan didn't back away, Brooke caressed Logan's cheek.
Logan closed her eyes and leaned into the touch, causing Brooke's
pulse to spike. She was playing with fire, but she didn't care. "And
beautiful, and dangerous."

"Dangerous?" Logan asked, her voice little more than a whisper.

"Just because I kiss you doesn't mean I want to sleep with
you." Brooke realized how utterly evasive and ridiculous it sounded
because she *did* want to sleep with Logan, but she went on without
missing a beat. "To me, sleeping with someone means more than a
night of fun and mutual satisfaction. You think about that, Logan, and
what it might mean for how you live your life. I'm not some woman
you—or anyone else—can pick up in a bar. You can't sleep with me
and never see me again. I live next door to you. Let all of it sink in
and then remember the things we've talked about. Neither one of us
is looking for a relationship, remember?"

CHAPTER TWENTY-ONE

Logan woke the next day on the couch with a tequila headache. She silently cursed herself for allowing Brooke to affect her to the point of drinking too much. She vaguely recalled Jack coming home around two in the morning and giving her a hard time for drinking the shit. Now he was sitting in their father's recliner facing her, a grin plastered on his face.

"What?" she asked tersely.

"Why can't you just admit you have feelings for her?"

"Who?"

"We're still playing that game?" Jack asked, rolling his eyes. He slapped her on the thigh on his way to the kitchen, which caused a burst of pain in the back of her head.

"Fuck, Jack." She pulled the blanket over her head and closed her eyes, willing the killer headache to disappear.

"The woman in question is Brooke Collier." Jack whipped the blanket off her a minute later and handed her a glass of tomato juice. "Drink this. It will make you feel better."

She eyed it—and him—with undisguised wariness before struggling into a sitting position. She sipped the tomato juice cautiously and was surprised to find it tasted good. She took a bigger drink and placed the empty glass on the coffee table. She gathered the blanket in her lap and turned her attention to him.

"What was it?"

"Bloody Mary with only half the amount of alcohol," he said with a grin. "Trust me, it got me through many a hangover in college.

Now, back to the topic at hand. Why won't you just admit you have feelings for her?"

"Because I don't."

"Bullshit. You were staring at her so hard in the bar last night I thought you were going to bore holes right through her head. What are you afraid of, Logan?"

"I'm not afraid. Jesus, why can't you just let it go?"

"Because you're my sister, and I want to see you happy."

"Trust me, Brooke Collier will not make me happy." Logan stared at the ceiling. "Fuck, we can't even spend more than an hour together before one of us is angrier than a hornet at the other one."

"That's called chemistry, you dope." Jack laughed, causing more pain to lance through her brain.

"No, it's called oil and water. It's called two people who really can't get along."

"Do you argue from the start, or do you argue when things start to get a little too personal?"

"When they get personal."

"So you argue in order to keep things from getting intimate. You argue to hide your true feelings from each other. That's chemistry, Logan. God, it's so utterly ridiculous."

"Why are you so infuriating first thing in the morning?"

"I figured if you didn't want to be disturbed you'd have found your way upstairs instead of passing out on the couch. Besides, it's almost noon." He pulled on his jacket before walking to the front door. "I'll leave you with the wisdom I've acquired over the past few years being a star football player and then I'll never mention it again. Playing the field isn't everything it's cracked up to be. I can't wait until Cynthia and I are sharing the same house because I *want* to have someone to come home to at night. I *want* to have someone who cares enough to ask how my day was. I *want* to have someone to curl up with in front of the television, and someone to hold me while I sleep. No one wants to grow old alone, Logan, because then there's absolutely nothing to look forward to."

She flopped down and pulled the blanket over her head again when he slammed the door on his way out. She never would have figured Jack to be a romantic. She grudgingly admitted it would be nice to have all the things Jack mentioned, but could it be possible with Brooke?

Why not Brooke? It sure as hell wouldn't be Gretchen, or any of the other women she'd had fun with over the years. She'd already admitted Brooke made her feel things other women hadn't. If she didn't care about her, then Brooke probably wouldn't be able to get under her skin and there would be no reason to argue, right?

"Shit," Logan murmured as she turned onto her side. She cared deeply about Brooke. She felt more alive around Brooke than she had in what seemed like forever. Brooke was someone she could see herself with a few years down the road. The thought alone should have been sufficient to scare her, but for some reason it didn't. And *that* scared her.

❖

Logan had just sat on the couch with a beer, intent on watching television for the rest of the night when the doorbell rang.

"Hi," Brooke said as she tried to look around Logan into the house. "Jack asked me to come over for something."

"For what?"

"I don't know. He just called, and he asked if I could come next door and help him with something."

"Jack isn't here. He left this morning for work and I haven't seen or heard from him since almost noon." Logan tried to shut the door, but Brooke held a hand out to stop it.

"Then why would he have asked me over?"

"I have no idea."

"Excuse me, I have a delivery for Logan Swift and Brooke Collier," said a man walking up the front steps. He was carrying a brown paper bag, and he looked back and forth between the two of them. He looked at Brooke. "I know Logan, so you must be Brooke. Jack sent me with this food for you, and a message." He read from a slip of paper in his hand. "Enjoy this meal together, and if you still can't manage to get along, I'll never do anything like this again."

Brooke looked at Logan, her mouth hanging open. Her first instinct was to believe this was Logan's doing, but after a little more consideration, she didn't think Logan had a romantic bone in her body. She decided to go with it. She hadn't had dinner, and the sadness in her grandparent's house was making it difficult to breathe. Logan, however, shook her head.

"No, Andy, whatever it is, I don't want it."

"It's Chinese. Your favorite." He waved the bag in front of her so she could smell it. "And I'm under strict orders not to leave until you both agree to share a meal together."

Apparently, Andy and Logan knew each other, but Brooke had never seen him before. She stood back and let them hash things out.

"Take it away and tell my asinine brother his scheme didn't work." Logan tried to ignore the way her stomach growled in response to the aroma.

"Pork fried rice, shrimp chow mein, General Tso's chicken. You sure you want to turn your nose up at it, Logan? He paid for it. All you have to do is enjoy it."

Brooke watched while Logan tried to stare him down. After a moment she ripped the bag out of his hands and dismissed him before turning around and going back into the house.

"Are you coming in for dinner or what, Brooke?"

Brooke closed the door behind her. It wasn't the most romantic invitation she'd ever had, but she'd take it. She didn't stop to think about why the summons—romantic or not—thrilled her.

"Who is Andy?" Brooke asked.

"What?"

"The delivery guy. Andy. I've never met him."

"He's a friend of Jack's," Logan said without turning around. "They were friends in high school. And he isn't a delivery guy. He's a firefighter. I'm sure Jack paid him handsomely to do this though."

"How do I know you didn't plan this?"

"Seriously?" Logan turned to look at her. "This was not my idea. You constantly remind me nothing will ever happen between us. You reject me at every turn. Why would I want to waste my time doing something this elaborate?"

"Maybe something like this would actually get my attention. But you know what? I never thought it was you anyway. You don't strike me as the type to do anything romantic like this."

"Trust me, I can be romantic if there's someone who inspires me to be."

Brooke felt the jab in her heart and began looking for the dishes. All this fighting was getting ridiculous. They just couldn't seem to meet halfway. Or at least Brooke couldn't believe in Logan enough to give it a try, no matter how badly she wanted to.

"Plates are in the cupboard to the left of the sink." Logan ripped the bag open and began placing the takeout cartons on the counter. Brooke handed her a plate and some spoons to dish the food out with. "I really hate that he knows how to get to me. Chinese food is my weakness. *Good* Chinese food anyway."

"So we're being forced on a date?" Brooke asked. She took a step back when Logan whirled around to face her, a spoon full of fried rice pointed at her face.

"Jack seems to think we like each other for some reason. And no one is *forcing* you to do anything. You're welcome to leave, you know. It just means more food for me." Logan turned back to finish loading up her plate as she talked. "If you're staying, help yourself to food and beverage. Just don't drink all the root beer. I'd hate to accidently give Shane a *real* beer."

Brooke stood there dumbfounded. She felt like an idiot for the way she'd reacted the night before. She looked at the food on the counter after Logan returned to the living room. She'd been close to making up her mind to leave, but since Logan seemed so indifferent as to whether she stayed or not, she began filling a plate up with food.

"Jack's an ass," Logan said when they were done eating.

"Because he bought us dinner?"

"No, because he forced us into eating dinner together."

"Nobody forced me to stay here, Logan. I stayed because I wanted to."

"Yeah?" Logan seemed surprised. She shot Brooke a wary smile, and it warmed Brooke's insides. "I know it doesn't seem like it, but I do enjoy your company."

Brooke blushed slightly and looked away as Logan gathered their dishes and headed back to the kitchen. Brooke was just allowing herself the luxury of wondering where the evening might take them when there was a loud crash in the kitchen.

"Fuck!" Logan yelled.

Brooke ran into the other room and found Logan on the floor, a hand to her forehead and blood seeping between her fingers. Brooke didn't even think before dropping to her knees and pulling Logan's hand away to get a better look at the wound.

"Do you have a first aid kit?"

"Upstairs bathroom."

Brooke grabbed a clean dish towel and had Logan hold it to her head before she helped Logan to stand and guided her up the stairs. She situated her on the toilet seat and began going through the medicine cabinet. There wasn't much there, and Brooke was worried she was going to need stitches to close the gash. She needed to get it cleaned out first so she could assess the damage more accurately. She prepared a clean washcloth with soap and warm water before turning to Logan.

"This is probably going to hurt a little. I'm sorry, but I need to clean it out before I can dress it. How did this happen?"

Her question had the desired effect, and Logan pulled the towel away when Brooke gripped her wrist lightly. The idea was to get Logan talking about how she injured herself so she wouldn't react as strongly when the washcloth made contact with the open wound. She dabbed the cloth around the wound but didn't come close to it yet as Logan began to talk.

"My fucking brother left his size fourteen clown shoes under the table. I guess I wasn't watching where I was going and I tripped over them. Fuck!" Logan winced and jerked her head away as Brooke finally touched the washcloth to the wound. "Damn it! Do you even know what the hell you're doing?"

"I guess one of the perks of your profession is you never have anyone ask you that particular gem of a question," Brooke said, trying to concentrate on getting Logan's head turned back toward her. Brooke smiled when she heard Logan chuckle. "I'm a nurse, remember? I'm pretty sure I know what I'm doing. I'm afraid you're going to need stitches though. We should get you to the hospital."

"Can't you do it?" Logan reached up and grabbed Brooke's wrist.

Brooke met her eyes and immediately regretted it. Her breathing quickened and she saw Logan swallow hard. Logan's other hand came up to touch her, but stopped when she apparently noticed all the blood on her hand.

"You don't like hospitals?" Brooke managed to ask.

"Not particularly. Do you have a way to stitch me up without having to drive thirty miles away?"

Brooke got to her feet. She held out another towel to Logan and motioned to her face. "Hold this to the wound. I'll run next door and get what I need. I'll be right back. Don't move."

She ran down the steps and out the front door, not giving a thought to what she must look like until she entered her grandmother's front door and heard the gasp coming from the couch. She looked down at herself and saw the blood on the front of her T-shirt for the first time. She grinned at her grandmother and shrugged.

"I told you I could wring her neck."

"Yes, you did, but I don't believe wringing someone's neck would cause so much blood loss. What are you two doing over there?"

"It's a long story, but she hit her head, and I need to stitch the wound."

"Oh, my God," Marlene said as she came into the living room from the kitchen. She stood there looking Brooke up and down. "Is it yours or someone else's?"

"Cool," Shane said. He gave Brooke two thumbs-up and walked around his mother to take a seat on the couch next to her grandmother.

"It's Logan's."

"She likes you," Shane said. "You probably shouldn't have killed her."

"You're all a bunch of comedians, aren't you?" She marched up the stairs to her room where she kept her medical supplies. She also grabbed a clean shirt and sweatpants to change into after she was finished with Logan's wound.

CHAPTER TWENTY-TWO

L ogan stood in front of the mirror in the bathroom, appalled at all the blood on her face and her shirt. She leaned closer to the mirror and slowly removed the towel Brooke had handed her. The blood wasn't exactly flowing any longer, but it was still seeping out at a pretty good clip. She closed her eyes and covered the gash again. This was going to leave a hell of a scar in the middle of her eyebrow. She'd probably have one whopper of a bruise too. She must have hit her head on the corner of the counter.

I'm lucky I didn't hit it a couple of inches lower. My damn eyeball would probably be rolling around on the floor down there. She jumped when she heard the front door slam, and she hoped like hell it was Brooke returning and not Jack coming home from work. She really didn't want to see Jack yet, but she did want to spend more time with Brooke.

"Sorry," Brooke said when she entered the bathroom again. "When people see this much blood on you, they tend to want to play twenty questions."

"No problem. Thanks for doing this, Brooke."

"You're welcome."

"I'm sorry about your clothes."

"Don't be. Now hold still for me."

Logan tried her best to not flinch when Brooke began cleaning the wound again, and she took the time to really study Brooke. She was beautiful; there was certainly no denying it. Maybe it was finally time for Logan to try another relationship. She knew her father was lonely the last fifteen years after her mother died, and she didn't want that. As much as she'd always told herself she was perfectly happy on her own, deep down she knew it was a lie. The one-night stands had never been truly satisfying, and even though Logan hated agreeing with her brother about anything, she realized she did want someone to come home to every night.

"Where'd you go?" Brooke asked with a gentle hand on her cheek. She looked worried, and Logan smiled in an attempt to allay her concern.

"Nowhere. Just thinking too much. My dad always told me I'd think any situation to death before I'd actually act on anything."

"Well, I'm done here, unless you want help cleaning up."

"I think I can manage." Logan grabbed Brooke's hand. "But don't leave, okay? It's still early. Maybe we could watch a movie or something."

"Sure. I'll just be downstairs."

"You know, this evening doesn't count as our date. We agreed that wouldn't happen until after the funeral tomorrow."

"I'm looking forward to our date." Brooke said. "I'd argue if you tried to pass this off as the date you asked me on."

Logan shut the door when Brooke left and leaned against the counter. It was crazy to be thinking what she was thinking, wasn't it? Brooke didn't want a relationship either, so what would be the point in even pursuing anything with her? Logan sighed as she wet another washcloth with warm water and began to remove the blood from her face. Just thinking about Brooke caused her stomach to flutter. That reaction to a woman hadn't happened since the day she first met Julie.

She sat on the edge of the tub and stared up at the ceiling. Brooke was different from any other woman she'd ever met. She'd made it perfectly clear she wasn't interested in a one-night stand and Logan decided she couldn't pursue her with the same bravado she used in the bars. Brooke was special, and the best thing to do was to simply allow their relationship to move along at its own pace. Forcing things with Brooke would definitely be a mistake.

❖

Jack walked into the house a little after eleven, which woke Brooke up. The DVD they'd been watching had finished long ago, and there was a blue screen on the television. Brooke felt a weight on her thighs and looked down to see Logan fast asleep, her head in Brooke's lap. Brooke met Jack's eyes and blushed at his smile.

"This really isn't what it looks like," she said quietly, trying not to wake Logan.

"It would be nice if it was," Jack said. He stopped in his tracks when he saw the gash above his sister's left eye. "What happened?"

Logan stirred at the sound of his voice but didn't wake up. Brooke held her breath when Logan's hand moved to her hip. Brooke tried to extricate herself from Logan's grasp, but Logan held on tighter and groaned quietly.

"Don't leave me," she mumbled sleepily. "This feels nice."

Brooke felt her cheeks flush again and decided waking Logan up would be best for all concerned. She placed a hand on her shoulder and shook her gently.

"Logan, Jack's home. I think it's time to wake up."

"No, I want to stay like this forever."

"Logan, please, wake up." Brooke fought to not show any outward signs of how turned on she was. Logan's head in her lap evoked rather erotic thoughts, and there was no way she wanted Jack to have any clue about it. She squirmed a little, causing Logan to open her eyes. Logan's head turned and she looked up at Brooke, a slow smile forming on her lips.

"Sorry, I must have fallen asleep."

Jack cleared his throat and Logan sat up quickly before wincing and placing a hand to her temple, her eyes closed.

"Are you all right?" Brooke asked, concern for Logan's well-being shoving all other thoughts to the back of her mind. "Does your head hurt? Damn it, I should have taken you to the hospital. You might have a concussion."

"Slow down, Brooke, I'm fine. I just sat up too fast and got a little light-headed."

"Will someone please tell me what the hell happened?" Jack asked, his irritation obvious.

"You left your damn shoes sticking out from under the kitchen table," Logan said. "I tripped over them and hit my head on the corner of the counter. Nurse Collier here stitched me up and we were going to watch a movie, but I guess I fell asleep. The last thing I remember is Gandalf arriving in the Shire."

"Damn, you couldn't even hang in there for the first half hour of the movie?" Jack shook his head and laughed at her. "Lightweight."

"This looks bad, Logan," Brooke said, tentatively placing a finger over the stitches. It was turning a dark shade of purple. "Are you in a lot of pain?"

"I'm fine. I'm more embarrassed than anything." Logan got to her feet and immediately swayed. Brooke stood quickly and put an arm around her waist to try to steady her.

"You need to go to bed and get some sleep," Brooke said.

"Yeah, you're probably right," Logan said, her arm going around Brooke's shoulders.

"Can I help?" Jack asked, the concern back in his tone.

Brooke should have said yes, should have had him take Logan up to her room, but before she could think about an appropriate answer, she spoke.

"I can handle it. You'll be here all night, right? She shouldn't be alone, and you'll need to wake her up every couple of hours or so in case she does have a concussion."

"Absolutely," he said. "My room is right next to hers, so I'll hear her if she needs anything. And trust me, I know all about concussions."

"Hello, remember me?" Logan asked. "I'm right here. You don't need to talk about me like I'm not even in the room with you."

Brooke didn't say anything as she helped Logan up the stairs and into her room. Logan had changed into sweat pants and a T-shirt before going down to watch the movie, so Brooke decided not to have her get undressed, which was probably safer for both of them. Once Logan was on her back in the bed, Brooke pulled a blanket over her and felt her head for any signs of fever. Logan's eyes opened and met hers, causing a skip in Brooke's heartbeat. She sat on the bed next to her to hide the fact her knees wanted to give out under the intensity of Logan's stare.

"You could stay here with me, you know," Logan said quietly. "I promise not to bite."

"Unless I ask you to," Brooke said quietly. She really wanted nothing more than to crawl into the bed next to her and hold Logan all night long. She knew it would be a bad idea, but it didn't make the longing any easier to deal with.

"Damn, I'm going to have to change my repertoire."

"Get some rest, Logan. I'll come by in the morning to check on you." Brooke started to stand but stopped when she felt Logan's hand on her wrist. She closed her eyes briefly and asked for the strength to resist her before looking back to Logan.

"Why can't you admit there's something between us?" Logan asked, her grip loosening. She moved her hand up Brooke's arm causing a shiver to run up her spine. "Why do you keep fighting it?"

"Because you don't want a relationship and even if I wanted a relationship, which I don't, I *won't* do casual, Logan. We'd be playing with fire."

"I'd never let you get burned," Logan said, and for a moment, Brooke believed her. Her expression was so open and honest, Brooke wanted to say *why not?*

Wendy was *why not*. Wendy had succeeded in making her never want to have another relationship with anyone ever again. After Wendy left, Brooke went through a period of time thinking *she* was the problem in all of her failed relationships. But upon further reflection, she realized the only thing she was responsible for was falling for the wrong women. Logan would no doubt go down into the same category, and Brooke wasn't interested in having her heart broken yet again.

"I'm not Wendy, Brooke. I would never do to you what she did."

"I have to go now," Brooke said. Logan propped herself up on one elbow and cupped Brooke's cheek in her other hand. Brooke wanted to pull away from her touch, but something held her back.

"What if I told you I wanted to try?" Logan held up a hand when Brooke looked like she was going to protest. "I know I said that before, and I told you I didn't mean it, but I did. Listen to me. I know I've probably given you the impression I sleep around, but I don't. Yes, I go to bars once in a while to find some company for an evening, but it really isn't very often. Since you've been here, I've gone out twice, and both times I came home frustrated and alone."

"Why?" Brooke asked, looking a little bewildered. "Why are you telling me this?"

"I don't want there to be any misunderstandings between us, and I need you to know it was you I wanted to be with both times. Whether you know it or not, you helped me to get through one of the worst times of my life. Having you around made me not think so much about what I'd lost when my father died. I enjoy spending time with you, and I really do want to get to know you better."

Logan waited while she watched so many emotions flit across Brooke's beautiful face. When Brooke's eyes finally closed and she leaned into the hand Logan still had cupping her face, Logan's heart began beating faster.

"You know the right things to say, I'll give you that," Brooke said when she opened her eyes again. "But how do I know you aren't just telling me the things you think I want to hear?"

"You don't." Logan lifted one shoulder before pulling her hand back and sitting up against the headboard. "That's the beauty of getting to know each other better. You can learn how to tell when I'm being sincere, and when I'm handing you a load of crap."

Logan sucked in a breath when Brooke leaned closer. She was tempted to grab her and just pull her over so Brooke was on top of her, but she managed to keep her hands to herself. She knew instinctively Brooke wasn't the type to be pushed into something. It seemed to take forever for Brooke to close the gap between them, but when she finally did, Logan closed her eyes and allowed Brooke to take the lead.

Giving someone else control wasn't as hard as Logan thought it would be. Or maybe it was simply easy because it was Brooke. Brooke made her feel things no one else ever had. Logan parted her lips when Brooke's tongue gently probed. She was surprised but didn't object when Brooke straddled her lap, never breaking the kiss. When they finally came up for air, Brooke seemed shocked to realize where she was. She tried to pull away, but Logan placed her hands firmly on her hips and held her in place.

"Please don't make up some excuse as to why this will never happen again." Logan spoke quietly, worried if she was too loud it might break the spell. "I just want to enjoy the moment here with you."

"No excuses," Brooke whispered. "I was only going to say there are too many clothes between us."

Logan didn't even try to hide her shock. She grabbed Brooke's hand when Brooke began to unbutton her own blouse. She questioned her sanity in that moment. She wanted this—more than anything. So why was she holding back now? She brought Brooke's hand to her lips and held them there for a moment.

"I thought you didn't want casual," Logan said, watching in fascination as Brooke's eyes darkened with arousal.

"Is that what this is?" Brooke asked, breathless. "Because if I'm being completely honest, it doesn't feel very casual to me."

"No, it doesn't to me either."

"Then are you sure you want to continue?"

Logan hesitated, certain the fear would take hold. The fear of letting someone in, of letting herself care too much about someone. But it didn't. Being with Brooke felt right somehow. It felt safe. She started to say as much, but Brooke was off the bed in an instant, obviously taking Logan's hesitation the wrong way.

"Brooke, wait," she said, trying to figure out how to fix the situation.

"No. I don't know what the hell I was thinking." Brooke straightened her clothes and ran her hand through her hair. "You're injured, and I'm acting like a complete idiot the night before my grandfather is to be buried. I need to be home with my family right now. We can talk about this some other time. You need to rest."

Logan stared at the door after Brooke was gone, wondering how in the hell things had gone downhill so quickly. Brooke had been right about one thing though, she had a funeral to take care of in the morning, and she hadn't thought about it all evening, which wasn't like her at all. Rather than running after Brooke, she decided a good night's sleep was in order. They could talk about things tomorrow, after the funeral was over.

CHAPTER TWENTY-THREE

L ogan, the service was beautiful," Marlene said as everyone was leaving the cemetery the following morning. "Your father would be so proud of you."

"Thank you," she said around the lump in her throat. She felt Jack's hand squeeze her shoulder gently and was grateful he was there beside her. "Let me know if we can do anything for your mother, all right?"

"That means more to me than I can ever say. I think having Brooke here to help her has done wonders."

"She does seem to be in good hands," Jack said.

Logan followed his gaze and saw Brooke holding Peggy's hand as Peggy tossed a handful of dirt onto the casket which had already been lowered into the ground. Logan's eyes teared up at the sight, but she looked away quickly, refusing to cry at the memory the scene provoked. She and her father had done the same thing at her mother's funeral. And then she'd done it at his. So much death…

"And I have to say, having *you* here seems to have done wonders for Brooke."

"I beg your pardon?" Logan was taken aback by the comment.

"Oh, come on," Marlene said as she hugged Logan. "I tried to get your father to set you up with Brooke months ago. He said he had no interest in meddling in your personal life. He did say it would warm his heart to see you settle down with someone like Brooke though."

Logan didn't know what to say. She looked at Jack, but he was absolutely no help because he was trying too hard not to laugh. Logan backhanded him in the gut before turning and walking away from them both. She was stopped a few feet away by Shane.

"Thank you, Logan. You did a wonderful job, and my grandmother is grateful for all your help, even if she hasn't actually told you herself."

Logan stared at the fifteen-year-old man-child who was a complete enigma. She put an arm around his shoulders and walked to Brooke's car with him.

"You're an amazing young man, Shane, and I hope you never change. The fact you're a complete gentleman is a testament to how well your parents have raised you."

"That's a nice bruise you have there above your eye. It's a very cool shade of purple."

"You should see the other guy," Logan said seriously.

"Are you all right though?" he asked when they reached the car. "Emotionally, I mean. You're not acting like yourself."

"I'm fine," she said, though she really was anything but fine. Her stomach fluttered every time she looked at Brooke, and she broke out in a cold sweat when she considered the possibility of Brooke never speaking to her again. That possibility, along with having lost both her father *and* Henry in such a short amount of time, seemed unbearable.

"What happened last night? When Brooke came home she went right to her room and wouldn't talk to anyone. Did you piss her off?"

Logan laughed. She couldn't help herself. Then she laughed again at the indignant look Shane gave her. She forced herself to stop and pulled him into a hug.

"I love how protective you are, and yes, I guess I did piss her off, but it was only a misunderstanding. I promise it will be corrected before the day is over. If Brooke will give me half a chance, that is."

"If Brooke will give you half a chance for what?"

Logan stiffened as she released Shane and turned to face Brooke and Peggy who had walked up behind them. It was Peggy who'd spoken, and she was now looking back and forth between Logan and Brooke. Logan felt like she was six years old again and had been caught with her hand in the cookie jar.

"Peggy, I'm afraid there's been a misunderstanding between Brooke and myself. I was merely telling Shane I wanted to clear things up with her, if she'd give me half a chance."

"Of course she will, won't you, dear?" Peggy asked with a sad smile.

Brooke looked at Logan as though she might strangle her the moment they were alone, but she nodded at Peggy. Logan coughed into her hand in an attempt to cover up the chuckle threatening to escape.

"Absolutely I will, Gram," Brooke said, her voice overly sweet. She kissed Peggy on the cheek before grabbing Logan's arm and pulling her in the direction of the hearse. When they were far enough away, Brooke stopped abruptly and spun Logan around. Logan had to fight to keep her balance. "What the hell was that all about?"

"Last night."

"You were talking about last night with Shane?"

"No, not at all." Logan scratched the back of her neck and looked at her feet. This wasn't going to be easy. She hadn't done much apologizing to women in her lifetime. Apologizing for saying something insensitive she was getting used to, but apologizing for not going after Brooke the night before to straighten out their misunderstanding was something entirely different. "Come back to the funeral home with me. I want to talk about last night."

"Now? You want me to leave my grandmother now? She just buried her husband, Logan. I need to be with her." Brooke turned to walk away, but Logan grabbed her arm and forced her to stop. "Let go of me. Now."

Logan didn't, and Brooke had the urge to slap her if that's what it was going to take for her to release her. Logan's grip relaxed slightly and Brooke pulled away before taking a few steps away from her.

"Please."

Brooke stopped. Never before had she heard one word hold so much emotion. She couldn't force herself to take another step. Maybe she should give Logan the rope she needed to hang herself. It would be interesting to watch her squirm. Brooke took a deep breath and turned back around.

"Fine. I'll go with you to the funeral home, but all we're going to do is talk, do you understand me? And you only have one hour before I need to be home to help Gram with the visitors I'm sure will be bombarding her the rest of the day."

"Not a problem."

Brooke walked back to her family to tell them what was happening before she got in the hearse with Logan. She tried not to think about all of the bodies the vehicle had transported over the years and swore she would never ride in another hearse again as long as she lived.

She closed her eyes and gave thanks to whoever was responsible for her not actually saying those words out loud.

❖

"You better talk fast, Swift, because you only have about half an hour before we need to head for home."

"I need to change. Please, come upstairs with me."

Her apartment was upstairs. Was this some stupid ploy to get her alone in the apartment? Logan wouldn't really be so conniving, would she? Brooke followed her up the grand staircase in the entryway. There were two separate doors there, and Logan took her through the first one, which happened to be her bedroom.

"You aren't planning on getting undressed with me in the room, are you?" Brooke looked around the bedroom Logan led her to and was impressed. The king-sized bed didn't even take up half the space. One entire wall was a floor to ceiling bookcase crammed full of books. The rest of the walls were adorned with pictures of family. She recognized Jack, and their father, John. The woman who looked so much like Jack could only be their mother. She'd been a beautiful woman. Brooke was startled when Logan spoke from right next to her because she hadn't heard her approach.

"I still miss her every day." Logan's voice was quiet and Brooke didn't object when Logan's hand clasped hers, their fingers intertwining. Brooke used the thumb of her free hand to wipe a tear from Logan's cheek. Logan pointed to a photo of her with Jack and their mother on what appeared to be Logan's high school graduation. "She was Jack's biggest fan. She was the one who encouraged him to pursue his dreams. If she'd lived, I'm sure she would have been one of those mothers who went to every one of her son's college games."

"She sounds like a wonderful woman."

"She was." Logan squeezed Brooke's hand before letting go. "I'm sorry she never got to meet you. I think she really would have liked you."

Brooke didn't know what to say. She watched as Logan looked down at her feet before turning to walk toward the bathroom. Brooke grabbed her hand and stopped her before leading her to the bed and sitting down.

"What did you want to talk to me about?"

"You misunderstood my hesitation last night," Logan said without looking at her. She stared at her hands clasped tightly in her lap. "It's been a long time since I've ever done anything other than casual. I expected panic to set in at any moment. That's why I hesitated."

"Panic? Why?"

"Because you make me nervous, Brooke. You make me feel things I've never felt before. Things I didn't think I'd *ever* feel. You deserve so much more than casual. I'm scared I won't be able to give it to you, and I'm scared to realize I want to try. I want to trust in having a tomorrow with you."

Brooke stared at her knowing her mouth was hanging open but physically unable to do anything about it. She felt her heart melt as the true meaning of Logan's words sank in. When Brooke finally managed to close her mouth, she found herself smiling, and it was then Logan finally looked at her.

"You think it's funny."

"No, I think it's incredibly sweet. I know it couldn't have been easy for you to say those things to me."

"But it was, and *that's* what scares me more than anything. I've tried pushing you away, which is why you always seem to be pissed off at me for one thing or another. It's a defense mechanism. But I've finally realized I'm miserable when you're mad at me. I want to spend time with you. I want to be the one you bitch to—not the one you bitch *about*."

Brooke felt tears well up in her eyes, and she fought to not let them fall. She took a deep breath before standing and pulling Logan to her feet. They stood facing each other for a moment, and she couldn't stop her eyes from darting back and forth between Logan's eyes and her lips. Logan seemed nervous, shifting her weight from her right foot to her left, but she never averted her gaze from Brooke's eyes. When Brooke was certain Logan was about to run, she placed a hand on the back of her neck and pulled her down for a kiss.

It was warm and gentle, and Brooke moaned at the feel of Logan's hands cupping her face. Logan was almost tentative—as if she were afraid Brooke might disappear from her grasp. When they pulled apart, Logan kept her eyes closed and sighed in what Brooke thought was relief.

"I was afraid you'd run screaming from the house."

"Would anyone notice?" Brooke asked with a mischievous grin. "It is a funeral home we're talking about here."

Logan's eyes opened and she smiled warmly. She tucked a strand of hair behind Brooke's ear then placed her palm on her cheek.

"I know you've had bad experiences with breakups in the past, but would you be willing to give me a chance? I promise I'll never do anything to hurt you intentionally." Logan waited for an answer, her breath held in anticipation of what Brooke's response would be. Brooke leaned in for a quick kiss before sitting down again. Logan allowed herself to be pulled down beside her. Her stomach fluttered when Brooke held her hand, their fingers entwining.

"Can I think about it?"

Logan's heart dropped as she looked away. Her eyes focused on the family picture they'd had taken before Logan left for college. It was the last picture taken of all four of them together, and Logan had placed it on the wall everywhere she'd lived since then. She found herself wishing her mother was there now.

"Hey," Brooke said as she placed a finger under Logan's chin and turned her head to meet her eyes. "I didn't say no."

"You didn't say yes either."

"You're the one who pointed out I've spent half my time since we met being pissed at you, right? I'd really like to see if we can get through an evening without that happening, okay? Can we try a date or two and see how things go?"

"Absolutely." Logan grinned and she felt like a weight had been lifted off her shoulders. "What are you doing tonight?"

"I need to be with my grandmother. You're welcome to come to the house with me if you'd like. Maybe we can go out for a bite to eat later, if Marlene doesn't mind."

"Give me twenty minutes to shower and change."

Logan's heart felt lighter than it had in months. There was an unbelievable sadness hanging over her at having lost not only her father but Henry too, but for the first time in years, she didn't dread what tomorrow might bring.

CHAPTER TWENTY-FOUR

Logan spoke with quite a few people over the course of the afternoon, but her gaze never strayed far from Brooke, who had been by Peggy's side from the moment they'd arrived at the house. She looked over her shoulder when she felt someone watching her. It was Marlene.

"Brooke tells me she might be having dinner with you tonight."

"If it's okay with you. She doesn't want to leave Peggy alone tonight."

"Shane and I will be here, so don't worry about it. Have fun."

"How long are you staying in town?"

"Since Shane's winter break is about to start, we're going to stay until New Year's Day. You'll be spending Christmas with us, won't you?"

"I think Brooke and I need to figure out if we can get along for an entire evening before I commit to something like that, Marlene."

"Please," Marlene said. "You two were meant for each other. Sometimes I think you're the only two people in the world who can't see it. Have fun tonight, Logan, but if you ever hurt her, you'll have me and Shane to answer to. We may not seem like much, but you don't want to mess with us, trust me."

"I wouldn't doubt it." Logan turned her attention back to Brooke, who was looking at her and smiling. After a moment, Marlene tapped her on the shoulder.

"I don't know how much she's told you, if anything at all, but she's had a rough year," Marlene said. Logan noted the protective tone in her voice.

"She told me." Logan put her arm around Marlene's shoulders and kissed her on the cheek before pulling her into a hug. "And if I ever meet the woman who shattered her heart into a million pieces, she'll have to answer to me."

"There's a long line of us for that ass-whooping, so you'll just have to wait your turn."

❖

"Can we go back to your apartment for the nightcap you mentioned?" Brooke asked when Logan pulled out of the parking lot at the restaurant later that night. When Logan looked at her, Brooke shrugged. "Too many people at home with Marlene and Shane at my place, and Jack at yours. I was thinking I might want to kiss you without an audience present."

"Yeah, we can go there." Logan drove the short distance with her hand on Brooke's thigh and a smile plastered on her face. She never would have thought she'd enjoy a date so much. They'd spent the evening with Logan telling funny stories about Henry Collier, and they were getting along. No fights, no disagreements or misunderstandings. It was as close to a perfect evening as Logan could imagine.

She led Brooke up the staircase to her apartment, but they went through the second door instead of the first, which caused Brooke to hesitate for a moment.

"There's more to the apartment than the bedroom?" Brooke looked around the living room in what could only be described as awe.

"I'll be the first to admit I don't cook, but have you ever been in someone's living space where they didn't have a kitchen? Or at least a refrigerator? Where do you think I keep my beer?" Logan knew the apartment was huge. The master bedroom alone was bigger in square footage than the entire first floor of her father's and the Colliers' houses combined. She'd tried to talk him into living in the apartment instead of her, but he didn't want to leave the house.

"I guess I didn't really think about it. I just assumed the bedroom was all there was."

"We can certainly stay in the bedroom if it's what you want, but I do have a living room, as you can see, along with a kitchen, an extra bedroom, and another full bathroom," Logan said as she wrapped her arms around Brooke's waist from behind and kissed her temple. She moved to her ear, where she sucked gently on the lobe before continuing. "Would you like to stay in the bedroom?"

"I can't think when you're doing this," Brooke said, trying to step away from her, but Logan held her tighter.

"That's kind of the point, you know?"

Brooke's body melted back into hers as she whispered the words close to her ear. Logan kissed her jaw when Brooke reached up and touched the back of her neck, applying just enough pressure to let Logan know exactly what she wanted. Logan loosened her hold so Brooke could turn in her arms, and they kissed. Logan didn't object when Brooke began unbuttoning her shirt, but when Logan felt Brooke's hand on her exposed flesh, she broke the kiss.

"Are you sure about this?" Logan asked, her voice strained.

"More than I've ever been of anything in my life." Brooke's eyes closed and she bit her bottom lip to stifle a moan when her fingers brushed across Logan's nipple.

"Jesus," Logan said in a strangled whisper. The nipple hardened immediately, and Logan felt like she might come at any moment. She grabbed Brooke's wrist to stop her movements and met her desire-infused gaze. "What about that nightcap?"

"I thought this was it."

"Oh, yeah, that'll work," Logan said before taking her lips in a kiss she hoped conveyed everything she was feeling. They both moaned when Logan pulled Brooke's blouse free from her pants and ran her hands up her sides underneath. Logan whimpered when Brooke pulled away from her and began removing her own clothes.

"Seriously, Logan, there are too many clothes in the way here," she said, her voice raspy with need.

Logan didn't need to be told twice. She made quick work of removing her clothing, but she faltered when Brooke's breasts were freed from her bra. She was worried she'd start salivating at the sight and moved to cup them both in her hands. Brooke smiled nervously when their eyes met.

"You are so beautiful," Logan whispered before bending to take a nipple between her lips. She wrapped her arms around Brooke's

PJ TREBELHORN

waist when she felt hands in her hair holding her firmly in place. They held to each other tightly as Logan stood up straight again, Brooke's legs going around her waist.

"Bed. Now."

Brooke clenched her legs around Logan's waist, her eyes closed and her head tilted back. The image was sexy as hell, and Logan wasn't sure her legs would hold them both upright for the walk to the bed, but she managed somehow. After placing Brooke gently on her back, Logan quickly removed her pants and boxers before she finished undressing Brooke. When she was done, she took a step back and admired the gorgeous body in her bed.

"Change your mind?" Brooke asked with a grin.

"No, not in a million years," Logan said before covering Brooke's body with her own. She smiled at the hiss that escaped Brooke's mouth when their naked flesh met along their lengths for the first time. Logan nuzzled her ear, causing a tremor to go through Brooke's body. "I need to be inside you."

"Yes. Do it, baby. I need to feel you now."

Logan rolled onto her side, causing Brooke to do the same so they were facing each other. She held Brooke's gaze as she moved her hand between their bodies, only slowing her progression when her fingertips brushed against the hair at the apex of Brooke's thighs. Logan grinned when Brooke closed her eyes and tried to forcibly push her hand lower to where she obviously needed Logan most.

"Don't tease me," she said, burying her face in Logan's shoulder and spreading her legs to give her better access. "Logan, I need you to fuck me."

"I don't want to fuck you, I want to make love to you. Will you let me?"

Brooke pulled back and looked at her. Logan sucked in a breath at the look of pure desire she saw. She moved her fingers slowly, relishing the wet heat as she entered Brooke's folds. Brooke shuddered under her touch but managed to cup her cheek momentarily.

"Yes, but please hurry. I feel like I might spontaneously combust if you don't go inside soon. You have no idea how long I've wanted this with you."

Logan entered her slowly with two fingers and watched Brooke's eyes slide closed. Her hips moved in rhythm with Logan's slow thrusts, and she made little moaning noises every time Logan's thumb made contact with her clit.

"Look at me." Logan's voice was commanding, and when Brooke didn't do as she asked, Logan stopped moving. Once Brooke finally opened her eyes, Logan started again, but even slower than before. "I want you to look at me when you come."

Brooke sucked in her bottom lip and nodded while moving her hips faster with each thrust, causing Logan's thumb to collide with her clit with more force. Brooke threw a leg over Logan's body, and Logan resituated herself so she was on her back. Brooke wasted no time straddling her, her hands on Logan's shoulders. Logan watched as Brooke moved up and down on her fingers, her clit rubbing against Logan's belly with each downward motion.

Logan felt the muscles contracting hard around her fingers a fraction of a second before Brooke cried out in pleasure. She fell forward so she was on top of Logan, her body still pressing down hard against her hand.

"Logan…so fucking good…please…don't stop."

Logan curled her fingers and pressed the heel of her hand against her clit as Brooke's walls tightened around her hand and she cried out again, her hips pumping furiously to milk all she could out of her second orgasm.

After a moment, her movements ceased, and she collapsed with a sigh on top of Logan. Logan chuckled when she whimpered in protest as Logan slowly pulled out of her. One last spasm gripped her fingers tightly before she was completely free. Logan wrapped her arms around her and held her.

"Are you okay?"

"I think all my bones have liquefied, thank you very much." Brooke didn't move at all, and Logan kissed her gently on the temple. "I hope you're proud of yourself."

"I am." They lay quietly for a long moment, both catching their breath.

Brooke lifted her head and looked at her. She'd never before had the sensation of being thoroughly sated, yet craving so much more. She caressed Logan's cheek with the backs of her fingers as she stared into her eyes. She smiled at the uncontrollable tremors that still shook her periodically as her body tried to recover from what Logan had done to it.

"You should be." Brooke felt her cheeks flush in embarrassment at her next words. "I've never had two orgasms before. And I've never come so hard."

"I'm honored to have been your first."

Brooke's first reaction was to laugh, but she could see the sincerity in Logan's eyes as she spoke. This wasn't a line she used on just anyone. Brooke felt as though someone truly cherished her. She'd never felt so much before, from anyone. Her heart swelled in her chest.

"Don't move. I want you just like this." Brooke kissed her quickly before sliding down her body and settling between her legs. Logan's eyes were hooded, and Brooke ran a finger slowly through Logan's wetness, causing Logan's hips to buck.

"Jesus," Logan said in a strangled whisper. She gripped Brooke's wrist and pulled her back up, shaking her head. "I'm not used to giving up control."

"I don't understand."

"I've always been the one in control in the bedroom."

"So you're a top?" Brooke cocked her head to one side. She still didn't understand what Logan was trying to say. Logan let out a frustrated sigh and turned her head away. It dawned on Brooke what Logan was having trouble verbalizing. She gently forced Logan to turn her head back toward her and waited patiently until Logan met her eyes. "You don't allow anyone to touch you, am I right?"

Logan nodded but didn't look away. Brooke took it as a positive sign and kissed her on the chin.

"Not ever?"

"Not since my ex."

"Baby, how do you…" Brooke faltered, not quite knowing how to say it. If she was doing the math right, her last girlfriend had been almost fifteen years ago.

"Get off?" Logan asked after a moment. Brooke nodded. "I usually just take care of it myself while I'm touching the other person."

"But you didn't do it tonight." Brooke wasn't asking. Even though she was busy enjoying her two orgasms, she was enough in tune with Logan's body to know she hadn't come. "Why?"

Logan shrugged and tried to look away again, but Brooke wouldn't let her. She placed her hands on either side of Logan's face and stared into her eyes.

"Please talk to me," she said quietly. "Don't shut me out. I desperately want to touch you, but if it isn't what you want, I would never force you."

Logan's stare was defiant, and Brooke was about to give up. She stopped herself when she saw Logan's expression soften. Brooke's throat constricted with emotion when she noticed the tears welling up in Logan's eyes. She used her thumbs to gently wipe the tears away.

"I want you in ways I've *never* wanted anyone before," Logan said, her voice so quiet Brooke had to actually watch her lips in order to really hear what she was saying. "I thought if I didn't let anyone touch me I could keep on being happy without someone in my life. It gave me pleasure to give pleasure, and I never let them get close enough to touch me. Then you had to show up, and everything I thought I knew about myself went right out the window. I *need* you to touch me, Brooke. I need you to make me come. It scares me to think about how much I need your touch."

The tears fell then, and Brooke couldn't help crying too. The emotions were too much to handle. Logan held her tightly and buried her face in Brooke's shoulder.

"Shhh, baby, it's okay," she whispered, holding Logan just as tightly. She murmured the same things over and over in an attempt to calm Logan, and after a couple of minutes, she stopped crying. "Are you all right?"

"I'm sorry. I wouldn't blame you if you wanted to go."

"You have nothing to apologize for, and you aren't getting rid of me so easily." Brooke kissed her neck and smiled when Logan groaned playfully. "Will you let me make love to you?"

"Yes."

"Tell me to stop if it gets to be too much." Brooke waited until Logan nodded her assent before kissing her throat.

Brooke moved down her body slowly, wanting to give Logan time to get used to her touch. When she closed her lips around an erect nipple and began to suck gently, she thought Logan might make her stop, but she was pleased to feel her hands on her shoulders, urging her to move farther down her body.

"Oh…yes," Logan rasped when Brooke's mouth made contact with the heated flesh between her legs.

Logan let her legs fall open and Brooke ran her tongue along her sex, eliciting a primal moan that caused a shiver to run down Brooke's spine. Logan's hips bucked when Brooke entered her with her tongue, and when she didn't ask her to stop, Brooke pulled out and covered her clit with her mouth. She sucked gently and slowly penetrated her with a finger. When Logan didn't object, she added another finger. She opened her eyes and saw Logan squeezing her own nipple and knew it wasn't going to take much to push her over the edge.

Brooke thrust into her while her tongue quickly flicked Logan's clit. She felt the muscles clamp tightly around her fingers, and Logan's body stiffened with her hips raised off the bed. When she finally cried out and went limp, Brooke crawled back up the bed to lie next to her.

"Oh fuck."

"Are you all right?" Brooke asked quietly.

"Better than all right." She put her arms around Brooke and pulled her against her body. Brooke settled her head against Logan's chest, amazed at how fast her heart was beating. "I can't find words to describe how I feel right now. But it's definitely better than all right. Thank you."

"You never have to thank me for doing something I want to do."

"I'll keep that in mind."

Brooke raised her head to look at the clock next to the bed, surprised to find it was almost midnight. Logan rolled them over so she was on top once again.

"You're mine for the rest of the night," she said, and Brooke's pulse spiked at the possessive tone in her voice. "If they haven't needed you by now, then they'll be fine until morning."

Brooke wrapped her legs around Logan's waist and pressed her center hard into Logan's pelvis, causing them both to suck in a breath. She kissed Logan as they began to move in unison. Brooke didn't think she could get dressed and go home now even if she wanted to. But leaving was pretty much the furthest thing from her mind.

CHAPTER TWENTY-FIVE

Logan woke at six the next morning. She tried to turn onto her side before she realized Brooke was there, one leg slung over both of hers, and an arm across her torso. She sucked in a breath when Brooke's hand moved up to cup her breast, and memories of the night before flooded her mind.

Normally, waking up with a woman in her arms meant it was time to make her retreat before said woman woke up. But Logan knew in her heart the last thing she wanted to do was run away from Brooke. She was definitely falling in love, and the thought scared the hell out of her. But nothing scared her more than the possibility Brooke wouldn't return her feelings.

She pushed the thought from her mind and worked at extricating herself from Brooke's grasp. When she was completely free, she stood and watched Brooke, a feeling of contentment washing over her. Brooke reached out in her sleep and Logan moved her pillow so Brooke latched on to it and wrapped it in her arms.

Her stomach growled, and she remembered she didn't have anything in the apartment to eat. After quickly getting dressed, she grabbed her keys and made the decision to drive in to Riverside to get some bagels and cream cheese. Before she left though, she placed a soft kiss on Brooke's lips. Brooke moaned and held tighter to her pillow, and Logan felt her sex clench in response. After the night they'd shared, the last thing she should want was more sex, but she couldn't seem to get enough of Brooke. She turned and left before she changed her mind and woke Brooke up.

❖

Brooke opened her eyes when she heard her cell phone ringing. She scrambled out of the bed and found her purse on the floor near the bathroom where she had dropped it the night before. As she stood with the phone in her hand she looked back at the bed and felt a pang of disappointment to find Logan wasn't there. A quick glance at the phone's display told her nothing. It was a restricted number. With a feeling of dread in the pit of her stomach, she answered the call.

"Hello?" She made her way back to the bed and sat down.

"Brooke?"

Brooke didn't recognize the voice at first, but then the feeling of dread quickly turned into panic when she realized it was Wendy. *Fuck.*

"Brooke, are you there?"

"I'm here. What do you want, Wendy?" She knew she should have gotten a new phone with a new number when she moved, but she hadn't heard from Wendy in months and thought she was through with her.

"I ran into your father yesterday at the supermarket and he told me what happened to your grandfather. Long story short, I'm in Oakville and I want to see you."

"You're in Oakville? What the hell, Wendy? What would make you drive all the way here from Philadelphia?"

Brooke held the phone to her ear as she tried to get her clothes on. She vacillated between being furious with her father for telling Wendy where she was and being irate with Wendy for having the gall to show up. There had been a reason she'd never brought Wendy to see her grandparents, and it had nothing to do with wanting to keep her sexuality a secret from them. It had taken her almost six months after Wendy left her to admit to herself it was because she'd known they weren't going to last. She'd never really been in love with Wendy.

"I want to see you." Wendy spoke in a tone that indicated she thought Brooke was a child, which only made her more livid.

"I *don't* want to see you," she said in the same tone. Fully dressed now, Brooke walked to the bathroom and then to the kitchen looking for Logan. Where the hell was she? She walked back to the bedroom and looked at the clock on the nightstand. She tried to ignore the feeling Logan might have woken up and regretted what they'd done the night before. "Jesus, Wendy, what would possess you to call me before seven o'clock in the morning?"

"I drove all night to get here. Please, baby, I need to see you."

"Baby? Really? After what you did to me, you have no right to call me that."

"I'm sorry. For everything. I'm in a little diner across the street from a funeral home. Wait, I'll tell you the name of it."

Brooke's heart beat faster as she waited for Wendy to go look, but she knew what she was going to say. She closed her eyes and prayed for Logan to come back.

"It's on Main Street, and the business across the street is Swift Funeral Home. Please, Brooke, I just want to talk to you. Will you come have breakfast with me?"

"I'll be there in a few minutes." Brooke ended the call without waiting for a response. She felt sick to her stomach. She didn't really want to see her, but hoped this was a way of getting rid of Wendy once and for all. The last time they'd seen each other, Brooke hadn't been ready to give up on them, but a lot had changed since then. *She'd* changed, and it was time to let Wendy know it. Why would she even be in town? It sure as hell couldn't be to offer her condolences on her grandfather's death, because it wasn't her style. Brooke let out a frustrated sigh and pulled a piece of paper out of her purse to write a note for Logan. She left it on the pillow before heading down the stairs and out the front door of the funeral home.

"It's so good to see you again," Wendy said. She attempted to hug her when Brooke walked up to the table, but Brooke pushed her away before taking a seat in the booth.

"I'm sorry about your grandfather."

"Thank you."

"I saw you come out of the building across the street. What were you doing at a funeral home so early in the morning?"

Brooke thought about lying, about telling Wendy there were loose ends with her grandfather's funeral, but what would be the point? Really, what Brooke did was none of Wendy's business, period.

"A friend of mine owns it and lives upstairs." Brooke nodded at the waitress when she stopped at the table with a coffee pot in hand.

"A friend?" Wendy asked, her tone suspicious.

Brooke thought it was ironic, since Wendy was the one who always lied. What right did she have to be skeptical about anything Brooke said? Wendy looked upset, and part of Brooke was extremely pleased at the reaction. She didn't respond as she poured some cream into her coffee.

"A *girl*friend?" Wendy finally asked when Brooke didn't respond.

"In case you've forgotten, you have no right to be upset if I'm seeing someone. You lost that right when you left me to get pregnant by sleeping with a man. *And his wife.* Are you all still one big happy family?" Brooke noted the way Wendy turned her head away and sat back in her chair. Apparently, the answer was no, and Brooke was thrilled to realize she didn't care. "I don't understand why you did things the way you did, and honestly, at this point, I don't even want to understand. The fact of the matter is, you left me and I've finally moved on. I'm happy. You need to do the same, so why the hell are you even here, Wendy?"

"I want you back."

Brooke laughed. She couldn't help it. Wendy looked hurt by her reaction, and it only made her laugh more. Could Wendy really have expected Brooke to welcome her back with open arms? People were looking at them and Brooke didn't care. When she finally managed to stop laughing, she leaned forward and spoke quietly.

"You were too late to get me back the first time you had sex with *him.* I'm assuming it was before you actually left me?" Brooke didn't wait for an answer because she knew what it would be, and she also knew Wendy would lie about it. It was what she did so well. "Maybe you wanted to try it out first to see if you were going to like it? We've been broken up for just over nine months, and the baby was born about eight weeks ago, am I right?"

Wendy's jaw clenched as she gazed out the window to her right. Brooke was trying hard not to lose her patience, but she didn't want to be there with her ex. She wanted to find Logan and spend the day doing the same things they'd done all night.

"Why isn't the baby here with you?"

Brooke watched in silence as Wendy folded and unfolded her napkin over and over. She started to speak a couple of times, but then shook her head and let out an audible breath. Brooke was getting tired of waiting and glanced across the street to see Logan running up the walk to the front doors of the funeral home, a grocery bag in her hand. Brooke wanted nothing more in that moment than to be back there with Logan in her arms. Making love. She closed her eyes to try to keep her mind from going there and took a deep breath.

"They threw me out."

"What?" Brooke looked at her—really looked at her—for the first time since she'd sat at the table. The waitress came by and refilled their coffee cups, but Brooke waved her away when she asked if they were ready to order. Wendy looked tired. There were visible bags under her eyes and she was too thin for just having delivered a baby. "Tell me what happened."

"They threw me out and won't let me see Lucy. That's her name," Wendy said with a smile so sad it almost broke Brooke's heart. "They're taking me to court to try to get full custody from me."

"They can't do that," Brooke said. It was the first thing to come into her mind, but of course they could.

"Yes, they can. He's Lucy's biological father. I think this is what they wanted all along. She couldn't have children." Wendy gripped Brooke's wrist. That was when Brooke saw the nasty cut which wasn't quite healed.

"Jesus, Wendy, what is this?" Brooke ran her index finger across the angry red gash. There'd been stitches, and it looked as though they'd been removed recently. "Did you try to kill yourself?"

"I was depressed after Lucy was born. I didn't know what I was doing. They've latched on to it and are using it to say I'm an unfit mother. The logical choice would be to give custody to the father."

Brooke stared at her in disbelief. The woman lied about everything. When they were together, it had been so easy to have the wool pulled over her eyes so to speak. It was easier to believe her than to argue. Not now. Now Brooke saw through everything. She wasn't completely heartless, and a part of her wanted to comfort Wendy. Brooke couldn't understand how anything could push a person to try to commit suicide. But she also knew Wendy didn't really want her back. It was simply a way for her to try to manipulate Brooke's feelings. She refused to allow Wendy to get under her skin again.

"Why did you come here and say you wanted me back? I know as well as you do you only want me to help you out of the shit pile you got yourself into. I can't do it, Wendy. I won't let you drag me into your mess. I have a life here. I was through with you before I moved up here, and I'm through with you now. So if your intention was for me to help you get your baby back, you're out of luck."

"But you know me better than anyone else, Brooke. You can help to convince the judge Lucy belongs with her mother."

Brooke stared at her for a moment before getting up and walking away, ignoring Wendy's pleas for her to reconsider. Not only had her heart healed from Wendy's betrayal, but she'd also given it to someone else. Someone who was waiting for her.

CHAPTER TWENTY-SIX

Logan took the steps two at a time. She'd started out to get bagels and cream cheese, but once she was in the store, she had the overwhelming desire to cook for Brooke. It was a frightening notion, but she'd bought eggs, bacon, bread to make toast, and pancake mix with maple syrup in case Brooke preferred it to eggs. She just hoped she wouldn't set the damn place on fire in the process.

The smile she knew had been plastered all over her face since the moment she'd awakened earlier faded away when she entered the bedroom and saw the note on her pillow. She sat on the edge of the bed and unfolded the note, trying to ignore the rising dread she felt in her chest.

Logan,
I'm so sorry I had to leave. Last night was amazing.
I'll cherish it always.
Brooke

Logan stared at the note for what seemed like an eternity before ripping it up and tossing it in the wastebasket.

"I'll cherish it always? What the hell is that?" She flopped onto her back and covered her eyes with her hands. It sounded like a note she'd leave for one of her one-night stands. It stung. No, it pierced her heart. She knew a brush-off when she heard it, or read it, as the case may be. "God, I'm a fool. I need to stick with women in the bars from now on. I've never fallen in love with any of them."

Admitting it out loud, even to herself, caused a pain in her chest so acute she worried for a moment she might be having a heart attack. She was really in love. There was no way around it. Brooke had come to town and, from the very first moment they'd met, had begun embedding herself in Logan's life. Even worse, she was in her head. And now her scent, her taste, her laugh, was in her head too.

Damn it, she hadn't wanted this to happen. In fact, she'd spent years perfecting the art of avoiding everything she thought might lead to anything more involved than a night or two with a woman. How could she have been so fucking stupid?

Then another thought entered her mind. Brooke had come to Oakville to help Peggy take care of her grandfather. He was gone now. Was Brooke going to pack up and move back to Philadelphia? Logan didn't think she could stand it if Brooke left now. *Damn it, I don't even want to be in love.*

She raked her fingers through her hair and closed her eyes when the truth hit her right in the gut. Before she met Brooke, she really *hadn't* wanted to be in love. She'd carved out a nice quiet little life for herself. Then Brooke showed up on her doorstep and turned everything upside down. Now she couldn't imagine *not* loving her. And that particular thought hurt her heart more than she'd ever thought possible, because Brooke obviously didn't feel the same way about her. If she did, she'd still be there. She wouldn't have left a note on the pillow. She wouldn't have yanked Logan's heart out of her chest and trampled all over it on her way out the door.

She needed to get out of there. She stood quickly and grabbed her keys before running outside to her car again. Maybe Jack could help her come to her senses.

❖

Brooke walked outside in time to see Logan getting back into her car. She wanted to call out to her, but Wendy was right on her heels, still begging her to help get her child back. She watched powerlessly as Logan turned the corner without ever taking her eyes off the road. She'd appeared angry, but why? Brooke had left a note, which was more than Logan had bothered to do.

"Damn it, now I'll have to walk home."

"I can give you a ride," Wendy said as she grabbed her arm, her grip incredibly strong.

Brooke pulled away with more force than she should have, and Wendy ended up on her ass. She started crying and Brooke felt like a heartless jerk. She helped Wendy back to her feet and was surprised when Wendy's arms went around her neck. Brooke held her for a moment, not knowing what to say. It was an uncomfortable situation, but she listened to Wendy's sobs without saying a word.

"Please let me give you a ride home. I'm sorry I bothered you. I should have known it was futile asking you for help."

"What kind of help did you expect?" Brooke mentally kicked herself for asking and implicitly agreeing to the ride home.

"Just to talk to my lawyer. Then he would determine if your testimony could help my case."

"Honestly, Wendy, there's nothing I could say to your lawyer that would help your case. I'm not sure Lucy would be better off with you."

Brooke watched while Wendy wiped her tears away and opened the door for her. Brooke knew her statement couldn't have surprised Wendy. She'd said as much when she'd first found out she was pregnant. When she first began to realize she really didn't want Wendy back.

She got into Wendy's car and they drove the couple of miles to her grandmother's house in silence except for the directions Brooke gave her. They sat in the car for a few minutes, Brooke wanting nothing more than to say good-bye and run to Logan. Her car was parked on the other side of the street, but apparently, she was inside already. It was just as well. Brooke didn't want Wendy to meet Logan. More accurately, she didn't want Logan meeting Wendy. For some reason, the idea of Logan seeing what a loser she'd wasted three years of her life with wasn't appealing.

"Can I please have my lawyer call you?" Wendy asked when Brooke reached for the door handle. "All you'd need to do is tell him I'm not a threat to myself or Lucy. Just tell him about the three years we were together."

"I don't think it's a good idea, Wendy." Brooke knew if the lawyer called she'd have to tell him how manipulative Wendy was, not only when they were together, but even now. How she lied about so many things. How she cheated on her and left her for the situation she was now fighting to get away from. They both jumped when there was a rapid knocking on the driver's side window.

Instead of opening the window, Wendy got out of the car. Brooke did the same a second later and ran around the front of the car when she saw Marlene pushing Wendy with a hand firmly to her shoulder.

"What the fuck are you doing here?" Marlene asked, looking every bit the mother trying to protect her young. That was when she noticed Brooke, who was trying to get between the two of them. "This better not be what it looks like."

"It's not."

"Then you need to start explaining, because all I know is you stayed out all night, and then you come driving up with this piece of shit," Marlene said with a wave in Wendy's direction and a disgusted look on her face. "And Logan arrived here alone a couple of minutes ago."

"Where is she?" Brooke glanced at Wendy who, to her credit, was trying to step back from Marlene.

"Inside with Jack I would imagine. She came to the door asking about you, but when I told her I hadn't seen or heard from you since the two of you left last night, she went right next door without telling me what happened."

"I need to see her." Brooke started toward the door to Logan's house, but Wendy stopped her.

"Brooke, I really am sorry for everything. Please reconsider letting my lawyer contact you."

"I said no, Wendy. I really don't think anything I could say to him would help your case." Brooke responded over her shoulder, determined to literally put Wendy behind her. Logan opened the door before Brooke could even raise her hand to knock. She saw the hurt in her eyes and Brooke's fingers twitched with the need to pull her into an embrace.

"Who is that?" Logan asked before Brooke could even think to act on her impulse.

Brooke followed her line of sight to Wendy, who was still standing outside her car watching them. Marlene was still giving

Wendy a piece of her mind, but Wendy obviously wasn't paying any attention to her.

"Wendy."

"Wendy?" Logan looked confused for a moment but her expression quickly turned hard again. "As in your ex? That Wendy?"

"Yes, she called me this morning and wanted to see me."

Brooke flinched at the flash of anger in Logan's eyes as she redirected her gaze to her. Brooke reached for her then, but Logan stepped back quickly.

"So you ran right out to meet with her?" The hurt in Logan's eyes was enough to cause a sharp pain in Brooke's chest.

"What? No." Brooke shook her head and tried to touch Logan's arm again, but she pulled away from her. "Logan, I woke up and you were gone. I didn't know where you went, or when you'd be back— even *if* you'd be back. I was only across the street in the diner. You came home but left again before I could get back over there."

"Your note didn't indicate you'd be coming back, Brooke. It was a good-bye, I know that. Are you getting back together with her?"

Brooke stared at her in disbelief. What the hell was going on here? A good-bye? Was she crazy? It had been the most mind-blowing sex she'd ever experienced in her life, and she was pretty sure it had been for Logan as well. Who in their right mind would ever want to say good-bye to that?

"Hello," Brooke said. She reached up and knocked a couple of times on the side of Logan's head. Logan looked pissed and took another step back. "In case you've forgotten, I live right next door. Good-bye could never be said in a note, Logan."

"She did it," Logan said with a pointed look at Wendy, who was still being given a stern lecture by Marlene.

"I'm not her," Brooke said, feeling her anger begin to rise as well. Did she really think Brooke had forgotten how the end of her relationship had gone? "And I know you aren't her either. Please sit down and talk to me, Logan. I need to say something to you."

"I need to get the fuck out of here," Logan said as she grabbed a coat hanging behind the door and put it on before locking gazes with Wendy. She pushed her way past Brooke. She intended to storm past Wendy too, but Wendy never broke eye contact with her. Logan stopped and leaned down so only Wendy could hear what she said. "If you *ever* hurt her again, you'll have to answer to me. Understood?"

Wendy nodded and swallowed audibly before Logan turned and crossed the street. She looked up to the porch and saw Brooke standing there with tears in her eyes before she started the engine and took off. She couldn't think about Brooke being hurt by anything she'd said. Didn't Brooke realize how wounded Logan was by the turn the morning's events had taken?

Logan drove without even thinking about where she was headed. She finally ended up in a place she'd often gone to think out her problems after her mother died. They'd spent many Sundays as a family at Presque Isle National Park, and it gave her some peace to think her parents might be there with her now. She looked out over the bay to where she could see the Bicentennial Tower in the distance and took a deep breath.

She'd really had no right to react the way she did. Hadn't she known all along Brooke was in love with Wendy? Still, it hurt her heart in a way nothing else ever had before. When it came down to it, even though Brooke had said she didn't do casual, Logan had been exactly that when Brooke's ex had shown up. She thought about the women she'd been with and winced. If this was what they felt, she really was a shit. She'd bought a bottle of wine when she'd gone to Riverside that morning, hoping she and Brooke might share it later in the day. It was the reason she'd taken so long to get back home. She'd waited for the liquor store to open. She grabbed the wine along with the corkscrew she'd purchased and headed to the end of the pier. She opened the bottle and sat down, her legs crossed in front of her, and took a drink.

Maybe by the time she finished the bottle she wouldn't care anymore. About anything.

"Jack, you have to have some idea where she went." Brooke entered the house without knocking. She'd had more than she could handle with Wendy, but she'd finally convinced her she wasn't going to help and sent her on her way. Hopefully, she was done with her for good. Brooke wasn't about to let Jack give her the cold shoulder too.

"She told me about the note you left her this morning."

"Okay," she said slowly. She didn't have the time to be embarrassed that he no doubt knew what they'd spent most of the night doing. It really didn't surprise her to learn Logan had shared the note with him. "Why did she think I was saying good-bye in the note?"

"You're a piece of work, aren't you?" Jack stood and walked over to her, forcing her to tilt her head back in order to keep eye contact. She found herself feeling grateful Logan wasn't as tall as her brother. "*Last night was amazing. I'll cherish it always.* Seriously? If that isn't a brush-off then I don't know what is."

"Jesus," Brooke murmured under her breath as she realized how the words must have sounded to Logan. "Jack, I didn't mean it like that at all, I swear. I meant that…well, that I'll always cherish our first time together. Not that it was our last."

"You should be telling her, not me."

"Believe me, I would be if I had any freaking clue where she was right now." Brooke wanted to punch something, an urge which was totally foreign to her. Instinctively, she knew it wouldn't be a good idea to take her frustrations out on a man who was more than twice her size. Instead, she walked to the couch and sat down. "Please help me find her. Do you have any idea where she might be?"

"Maybe." He sat on the coffee table facing her, his eyes never leaving hers. "Tell me why you left the way you did this morning. She only went to the grocery store to get something to cook for you for breakfast. You have no idea what a big deal that is for her."

Brooke told him everything from the moment she'd been awakened by her phone until she'd ended up on the couch there with him. When she was done she waited for him to reply, but he just shook his head.

"So you really weren't giving her the brush-off?"

"God, no."

"Then why didn't you say *call me*, or something that may have been equally indicative of how you felt about the night you shared? Something that made it clear you wanted to see her again?"

"It was a freaking note! I wrote the first thing I thought of. I thought she'd know how I felt about the night we shared." Brooke had never been so frustrated in her life. She stared at her feet for a moment and couldn't believe she was actually going to tell him before she had a chance to talk to Logan, but it was the only way she could think of to get him to help her find her. She took a deep breath. "I love her, Jack. I love her, and I need to tell her that because she thinks I'm going back to Wendy, and believe me, that's the last thing I want to do. Please help me."

Jack got up and left the room without a word. Brooke dropped her head into her hands and sobbed. Jesus, was it really over with Logan before it truly began? She couldn't stand the thought Logan was out there somewhere in pain because of something she'd done. How could Logan not know what she was feeling after the things they'd shared the night before? Why hadn't she just told her she loved her? When Jack didn't come right back, she walked slowly toward the front door, assuming he wasn't going to help her. Just before she opened the door, he walked back in.

"Where are you going? I wrote down directions for where I think she probably is. I tried calling her, but she isn't answering her cell phone. You should try too."

"I did before I came inside. I know she won't answer a call from me right now." Brooke took the piece of paper he was holding out to her and then hugged him tightly. "Thank you, Jack. If you hear from her, please call me."

"I will. And if she comes back I'll tie her to a kitchen chair and keep her here."

"Thank you." She got up on her tiptoes and pulled him down so she could kiss him on the cheek. "Cynthia is a lucky woman to have found someone like you, Jack Swift."

She ran out the door and got into her car, dialing her grandmother's number as she went so she could let Marlene know where she was going. As she put the car in gear, she glanced at the directions Jack had given her.

Presque Isle? She'd never heard of it. She stepped on the gas and cursed the fact she'd never bothered to invest in a GPS.

CHAPTER TWENTY-SEVEN

L ogan heard a car door slam, but she didn't pay any attention to it. She'd looked the first few times it had happened, wondering if Jack had figured out where she'd gone, but it was always someone she didn't know. Christmas was only a week away, and it was freezing outside. Why the hell were there so many people out here? She glanced at the bottle of wine sitting on the pier next to her. She'd only taken a few sips out of it before she felt it sour in her stomach.

Footsteps behind her caused a shiver to run up her spine, and she shoved her hands in her pockets in an attempt to warm herself.

"It's freezing out here."

Logan's breath caught in her throat at the sound of Brooke's voice. Her first thought was she was going to kill Jack for giving away the one place she felt safe. She sat up straighter but didn't turn around—didn't say anything in response.

"I brought a blanket."

Logan closed her eyes tightly in the hopes it would stop her tears from falling. Frozen tears couldn't be good. She knew pretending Brooke wasn't really there couldn't be good either, but she continued her silence anyway. When Brooke sighed audibly behind her, she almost turned around. Almost.

"Logan, please, I've been calling you almost nonstop since the second I started driving here."

"I know. I ignored your calls, and Jack's too."

Logan refused to look, even when Brooke sat next to her so close they were almost touching. She fought the urge to wrap her arm around Brooke's shoulder and pull her closer so they could both be warmer.

"I thought maybe it would be a good indicator to both of you I'm not in the mood to talk," Logan said, her eyes on the Bicentennial Tower across the bay.

"I kind of figured as much."

"And yet here you are."

"Logan, I need to explain something to you. I didn't leave this morning because I wanted to. I left because I didn't know when you were going to be back, or even where you went. You didn't leave a note. The thought crossed my mind you might have woken up and regretted what happened between us."

Logan did finally turn her head then, but Brooke was looking at something in the opposite direction. Her stomach fluttered at the realization Brooke could possibly think she was still that person. The kind of person who would run away in the dead of night to avoid waking up next to a woman. The kind of person she'd stopped being the moment Brooke had come into her life.

"Are you fucking serious? After everything I said to you last night—everything we *did*—you really thought I didn't want to face you this morning? I let you touch me, which is a small miracle in itself. We were in my apartment. I told you before I'd never taken a woman there. It makes it pretty much impossible to accomplish the whole avoidance thing."

"Then I don't understand why you even took me there in the first place."

"Really? You don't get it?" Logan waited until Brooke looked at her and she smiled sadly. "You're different than any woman I've ever met. You're beautiful, you're feisty as hell when it comes to defending your family, and you make me want things I never wanted before. Damn it, you make me *feel*. I woke up this morning and had the undeniable urge to make breakfast for you. That's not something I do even for myself."

"Gee, and I thought it was just because I asked you to take me there." Brooke shoved a hand into Logan's pocket and held her hand.

"There's that too."

"Look, I woke up and you were gone. Wendy called and wanted to see me, and because she was in the diner across the street, I decided to go and see what she wanted. I saw it as a way to get rid of her. To close that chapter in my life. I wanted there to be absolutely nothing between us, Logan. I wanted to have a fresh start."

Logan wanted to believe her. After a slight hesitation, she pulled her hand away so she could put her arm around Brooke and pulled Brooke's body against hers, Brooke's head resting on her shoulder. She breathed in her scent, expecting to smell her citrus shampoo, but the scent she caught instead caused flashbacks of the night before. Her thighs tightened at the memory. "You smell like sex."

"So do you." Brooke giggled and buried her face in Logan's neck, breathing deeply. "But you know what? I love this scent on you."

Logan's heart soared, but then plummeted just as quickly when she remembered why she was out here in the freezing cold in the first place. Brooke said the right things before, but she'd never said she wasn't still in love with her ex.

"What about Wendy?"

"No, not so much on her."

Logan stiffened, not appreciating the humor at the moment. "I'm serious. Where is she?"

"I'm serious too." Brooke pulled away from her and looked her in the eye. "As far as I know, she's on her way back to Philadelphia. Honestly? I don't care where she is as long as I don't ever have to deal with her again."

"I thought you were still in love with her."

"I never told you that. I let you assume it because at the time we talked about her, I had no idea what was going to happen between you and me. Logan, I stopped loving her a long time ago. Probably before she even left me. I just didn't know it at the time, and I let my pride get in the way." Brooke snuggled closer to her. "I have to admit I am in love with someone else though."

"Oh, really?" Logan asked with a grin. She picked up the bottle and took another sip before offering it to Brooke. "What's her name?"

"Logan," Brooke answered with a grin of her own. "Just don't ask me when it happened, because in the beginning, you exasperated me something awful."

"You love me? Really?" Even though she knew Brooke had been referring to her, it still felt surreal to hear her say it out loud. Until that moment, Logan hadn't dared to even hope Brooke felt so much for her, but she felt a little light-headed at the declaration. Logan got to her feet and held a hand out to help Brooke stand.

"Yes, I do."

"How can you not know when it happened? I know exactly when it happened for me."

"Is this your way of saying you love me too?"

"It absolutely is. I love you, Brooke Collier." She placed a hand on Brooke's cheek.

"Maybe it was when you were so caring and tender with my grandmother at the hospital when my grandfather died," Brooke said. She took Logan's hand and rubbed it vigorously in a blatant attempt to warm it up. "Or maybe it was the way you were the voice of reason for Ray and Missy the night Billy came out to them. It might have been the day you helped my grandfather when he was having an Alzheimer episode."

"For me, it was the first day we met. You looked so scared when I mentioned Henry had a shotgun, I wanted to hold you and assure you I would never let anything bad happen to you." Logan placed her hands on Brooke's cheeks and moved so they were only a couple inches apart. "I do love you, Brooke. I just hope you'll give me the opportunity to prove I'm worthy of your love."

When Logan tried to close the remaining gap between them, Brooke placed a hand on her chest and pushed her back. When she tried to step back farther, Brooke held tightly to the lapels of her jacket.

"As much as I really want to kiss you right now, the cold is making my nose run, and I can only imagine how devastatingly sexy *that* probably is. Let's go home."

"Which home?" Logan asked. "Yours, mine, or my apartment?"

"Your apartment alone with you is where I want to be right now, but I think we should let Jack and everyone else know we're okay first. Then we can go back to your apartment. I think we should take advantage of the fact Marlene will be here through the end of the year to keep an eye on Gram."

"About that," Logan said, cursing the fact her insecurities were making themselves known. "With Henry gone, there's no reason for you to stay in Oakville. Are you going to leave?"

"Do you honestly think that? After what we just talked about? You're a very real reason for me to stay, and even if this hadn't happened between us, I don't think I could leave Gram anytime soon. After almost sixty years together, it isn't going to be easy for her."

"I think I just wanted to hear you say I was your reason for staying here," Logan said with a grin she was sure was just as goofy as the one Jack had the day Logan met Cynthia.

"Okay, that's settled. Can we go home now?"

"Yes. Let's hurry." Logan took off toward the parking lot at a dead run. Brooke passed her just before they got there. Logan bent over at the waist, her hands on her knees. "Damn, I better get in shape if I'm going to be hanging out with you."

"I have a very strict workout regimen planned for you. You'll be in shape in no time."

"I can't wait to start."

"Oh, before we get involved with other things, Gram wanted me to invite you, Jack, and Cynthia over for Christmas."

"I can't speak for Jack and Cynthia, but I would love to be there. I can't imagine spending the day—and all of my days—anywhere but with you."

Chapter Twenty-eight

L ogan stood in the doorway of the kitchen watching Brooke and Peggy put the finishing touches on their Christmas dinner. They'd invited Billy to join them, but Logan was surprised when he told her Ray had insisted he *and* his boyfriend have dinner with them. She hoped everything was going well in the Best household. Logan tried to convince Peggy they should all go out to dinner, but Peggy was adamant Henry would have wanted them all together under his roof.

A quick glance over her shoulder into the dining room was bittersweet. Henry's place at the head of the table was empty. Shane had done as his grandmother asked and not put a plate and silverware for that seat. When Logan turned back to the kitchen, Brooke was standing in front of her, her head cocked to one side and a lopsided smile on her face.

"Are you all right?"

"Yeah. Just wishing my father and Henry were here to join in the festivities."

Brooke placed a hand on the center of Logan's chest. Jack and Shane entered through the front door laughing. They'd been outside engaged in a snowball fight. Logan ignored them and held Brooke's gaze.

"So do I," Brooke said softly. "But on some level, I think they are here. I think they will always be here with us."

Logan lifted Brooke's hand and placed a lingering kiss on her palm before grabbing her around the waist and pulling her close. She pointed up to the mistletoe hanging above them.

"That thought makes me happy, but I hope they won't *always* be with us, if you know what I mean."

"I think they'll be courteous enough to give us some privacy." Brooke stood on her tiptoes and met Logan's lips in one of the sweetest kisses Logan had ever experienced.

"Geez, you two, get a room or something," Jack said from behind Logan.

"Can't let the mistletoe go to waste, little bro."

"Everyone, sit down. Dinner's ready." Peggy pushed past them and carried the turkey to the table. She handed the carving knife to Jack, but once everyone was seated, he placed it on the table in front of him and glanced at Cynthia.

"I'd like to say something before we get started."

"Is something wrong, dear?" Peggy asked, the concern evident in her tone.

Logan watched her brother, pretty sure what it was he was about to announce if the flush on Cynthia's cheeks were any indication. She was happy for them, but a part of her was saddened by the thought they were all moving on with their lives. It hurt so much to know their father was missing this.

"No, Peggy, nothing's wrong. This morning I asked Cynthia to marry me."

"Was she smart enough to turn you down?" Logan asked.

"Funny. You'll forgive me if I forget to laugh at your little joke. She said yes, and we've started construction on a new house about ten miles south of here." He directed his attention to Logan. "We'll be able to move into the house in about six months, so I'll need to stay next door until then, if it's all right with you."

"You don't even have to ask." Logan hugged him before giving Cynthia a quick kiss on the cheek. She took Brooke's hand under the table when she resumed her seat. Jack started carving the turkey and everyone began talking at once, congratulating the happy couple on their engagement.

Logan watched in silence, the stark realization she was entering a new chapter in her life striking quickly. Brooke gave her hand a squeeze and she knew she'd have good company going down that road.

About the Author

PJ Trebelhorn was born and raised in the greater metropolitan area of Portland, Oregon. Her love of sports—mainly baseball and ice hockey—was fueled in part by her father's interests. She likes to brag about the fact her uncle managed the Milwaukee Brewers for five years, and the Chicago Cubs for one year.

PJ now resides in western New York with Cheryl, her partner of many years, and their menagerie of pets—four cats and one very neurotic dog. When not writing or reading, PJ spends way too much time on the Internet and watching television and movies.

Books Available from Bold Strokes Books

Trusting Tomorrow by PJ Trebelhorn. Funeral director Logan Swift thinks she's perfectly happy with her solitary life devoted to helping others cope with loss until Brooke Collier moves in next door to care for her elderly grandparents. (978-1-60282-891-9)

Forsaking All Others by Kathleen Knowles. What if what you think you want is the opposite of what makes you happy? (978-1-60282-892-6)

Exit Wounds by VK Powell. When Officer Loane Landry falls in love with ATF informant Abigail Mancuso, she realizes that nothing is as it seems—not the case, not her lover, not even the dead. (978-1-60282-893-3)

Dirty Power by Ashley Bartlett. Cooper's been through hell and back, and she's still broke and on the run. But at least she found the twins. They'll keep her alive. Right? (978-1-60282-896-4)

The Rarest Rose by I. Beacham. After a decade of living in her beloved house, Ele disturbs its past and finds her life being haunted by the presence of a ghost who will show her that true love never dies. (978-1-60282-884-1)

Code of Honor by Radclyffe. The face of terror is hard to recognize—especially when it's homegrown. The next book in the Honor series. (978-1-60282-885-8)

Does She Love You by Rachel Spangler. When Annabelle and Davis find out they are both in a relationship with the same woman, it leaves them facing life-altering questions about trust, redemption, and the possibility of finding love in the wake of betrayal. (978-1-60282-886-5)

The Road to Her by KE Payne. Sparks fly when actress Holly Croft, star of UK soap Portobello Road, meets her new on-screen love interest, the enigmatic and sexy Elise Manford. (978-1-60282-887-2)

Shadows of Something Real by Sophia Kell Hagin. Trying to escape flashbacks and nightmares, ex-POW Jamie Gwynmorgan stumbles into the heart of former Red Cross worker Adele Sabellius and uncovers a deadly conspiracy against everything and everyone she loves. (978-1-60282-889-6)

Date with Destiny by Mason Dixon. When sophisticated bank executive Rashida Ivey meets unemployed blue collar worker Destiny Jackson, will her life ever be the same? (978-1-60282-878-0)

The Devil's Orchard by Ali Vali. Cain and Emma plan a wedding before the birth of their third child while Juan Luis is still lurking, and as Cain plans for his death, an unexpected visitor arrives and challenges her belief in her father, Dalton Casey. (978-1-60282-879-7)

Secrets and Shadows by L.T. Marie. A bodyguard and the woman she protects run from a madman and into each other's arms. (978-1-60282-880-3)

Change Horizon: Three Novellas by Gun Brooke. Three stories of courageous women who dare to love as they fight to claim a future in a hostile universe. (978-1-60282-881-0)

Scarlet Thirst by Crin Claxton. When hot, feisty Rani meets cool, vampire Rob, one lifetime isn't enough, and the road from human to vampire is shorter than you think… (978-1-60282-856-8)

Battle Axe by Carsen Taite. How close is too close? Bounty hunter Luca Bennett will soon find out. (978-1-60282-871-1)

Improvisation by Karis Walsh. High school geometry teacher Jan Carroll thinks she's figured out the shape of her life and her future, until graphic artist and fiddle player Tina Nelson comes along and teaches her to improvise. (978-1-60282-872-8)

For Want of a Fiend by Barbara Ann Wright. Without her Fiendish power, can Princess Katya and her consort Starbride stop a magic-wielding madman from sparking an uprising in the kingdom of Farraday? (978-1-60282-873-5)

Broken in Soft Places by Fiona Zedde. The instant Sara Chambers meets the seductive and sinful Merille Thompson, she falls hard, but knowing the difference between love and a dangerous, all-consuming desire is just one of the lessons Sara must learn before it's too late. (978-1-60282-876-6)

Healing Hearts by Donna K. Ford. Running from tragedy, the women of Willow Springs find that with friendship, there is hope, and with love, there is everything. (978-1-60282-877-3)

Desolation Point by Cari Hunter. When a storm strands Sarah Kent in the North Cascades, Alex Pascal is determined to find her. Neither imagines the dangers they will face when a ruthless criminal begins to hunt them down. (978-1-60282-865-0)

I Remember by Julie Cannon. What happens when you can never forget the first kiss, the first touch, the first taste of lips on skin? What happens when you know you will remember every single detail of a mysterious woman? (978-1-60282-866-7)

The Gemini Deception by Kim Baldwin and Xenia Alexiou. The truth, the whole truth, and nothing but lies. Book six in the Elite Operatives series. (978-1-60282-867-4)

Scarlet Revenge by Sheri Lewis Wohl. When faith alone isn't enough, will the love of one woman be strong enough to save a vampire from damnation? (978-1-60282-868-1)

Ghost Trio by Lillian Q. Irwin. When Lee Howe hears the voice of her dead lover singing to her, is it a hallucination, a ghost, or something more sinister? (978-1-60282-869-8)

The Princess Affair by Nell Stark. Rhodes Scholar Kerry Donovan arrives at Oxford ready to focus on her studies, but her life and her priorities are thrown into chaos when she catches the eye of Her Royal Highness Princess Sasha. (978-1-60282-858-2)

The Chase by Jesse J. Thoma. When Isabelle Rochat's life is threatened, she receives the unwelcome protection and attention of bounty hunter Holt Lasher who vows to keep Isabelle safe at all costs. (978-1-60282-859-9)

The Lone Hunt by L.L. Raand. In a world where humans and praeterns conspire for the ultimate power, violence is a way of life... and death. A Midnight Hunters novel. (978-1-60282-860-5)

The Supernatural Detective by Crin Claxton. Tony Carson sees dead people. With a drag queen for a spirit guide and a devastatingly attractive herbalist for a client, she's about to discover the spirit world can be a very dangerous world indeed. (978-1-60282-861-2)

Beloved Gomorrah by Justine Saracen. Undersea artists creating their own City on the Plain uncover the truth about Sodom and Gomorrah, whose "one righteous man" is a murderer, rapist, and conspirator in genocide. (978-1-60282-862-9)

Cut to the Chase by Lisa Girolami. Careful and methodical author Paige Cornish falls for brash and wild Hollywood actress Avalon Randolph, but can these opposites find a happy middle ground in a town that never lives in the middle? (978-1-60282-783-7)

More Than Friends by Erin Dutton. Evelyn Fisher thinks she has the perfect role model for a long-term relationship, until her best friends, Kendall and Melanie, split up and all three women must reevaluate their lives and their relationships. (978-1-60282-784-4)

Every Second Counts by D. Jackson Leigh. Every second counts in Bridgette LeRoy's desperate mission to protect her heart and stop Marc Ryder's suicidal return to riding rodeo bulls. (978-1-60282-785-1)

Dirty Money by Ashley Bartlett. Vivian Cooper and Reese DiGiovanni just found out that falling in love is hard. It's even harder when you're running for your life. (978-1-60282-786-8)

Sea Glass Inn by Karis Walsh. When Melinda Andrews commissions a series of mosaics by Pamela Whitford for her new inn, she doesn't expect to be more captivated by the artist than by the paintings. (978-1-60282-771-4)